W9-BPG-092

ARF

ARF

A BOWSER AND BIRDIE NOVEL

SPENCER QUINN

Copyright © 2016 by Pas de Deux Corp

All rights reserved. Published by Scholastic Press, an imprint of Scholastic Inc., *Publishers since 1920*. SCHOLASTIC, SCHOLASTIC PRESS, and associated logos are trademarks and/or registered trademarks of Scholastic Inc.

The publisher does not have any control over and does not assume any responsibility for author or third-party websites or their content.

No part of this publication may be reproduced, stored in a retrieval system, or transmitted in any form or by any means, electronic, mechanical, photocopying, recording, or otherwise, without written permission of the publisher. For information regarding permission, write to Scholastic Inc., Attention: Permissions Department, 557 Broadway, New York, NY 10012.

This book is a work of fiction. Names, characters, places, and incidents are either the product of the author's imagination or are used fictitiously, and any resemblance to actual persons, living or dead, business establishments, events, or locales is entirely coincidental.

Library of Congress Cataloging-in-Publication Data available

ISBN 978-0-545-64334-4

10 9 8 7 6 5 4 3 2 1   16 17 18 19 20

Printed in the U.S.A.   23
First edition, May 2016

Book design by Kristina Iulo and Elizabeth B. Parisi

TO GABRIELLA

one

I AWOKE TO THE SMELL OF BACON. COULD THE day have gotten off to a better start? Not to my way of thinking, even though I knew right away that this bacon was of the distant kind, not sizzling in our own kitchen here at 19 Gentilly Lane, but somewhere in the neighborhood. Certain smells—bacon, for example—have the power to pull you toward them. With your tiny nose—compared to mine, that is—this may be news to you. It's not your fault! Don't feel bad!

I sprang off the bed, glanced back at Birdie. She was fast asleep, hair all in a tangle, crust in the corners of her eyes, and a bit of drool leaking from the side of her mouth. No one was more beautiful than Birdie. There are times when I can just gaze at her for what seems like forever. This wasn't one of them.

I trotted out of our bedroom, bacon pulling me along nose-first down the hall. I went by Mama's bedroom, empty until a few days ago. But now Mama was back from some faraway job and I could hear her breathing, slow and deep. Next came the kitchen and the door to the outside

1

world. Closed, of course. I looked across the breezeway that led to Grammy's part of the house, also closed. Around then was when I became aware of how faint the daylight was, meaning it was still kind of early. I turned to the window that faced the street and stared at the outdoor world, smelling bacon and thinking about nothing at all. With the exception of bacon.

A car came up the street, headlights on until it got close to our place, and then switched off. The car was one of those sporty two-seaters. The first thing I noticed was the cat curled up on the shelf in back, by the rear window. This cat, golden in color and fluffed up to the max, looked very comfortable. That annoyed me. The next thing I knew I was up on my hind legs, both front paws pressing on the glass. The car slowed down and the driver turned and took a long look at our house, scanning it from one end to the other. I had no interest in the driver—the cat had all my attention. But something about the way he was checking out our place, meaning mine and Birdie's, and I suppose Grammy's and Mama's, too, reminded me who was in charge of security at 19 Gentilly Lane. Namely me, ol' Bowser. That meant forcing my gaze away from the cat and laying it smack on the driver.

Some humans think they're pretty hot stuff. This driver was one of them. You could tell by the tilt of his head, like he was above it all. His thick hair was similar in color to the cat's; he also had a thin mustache that was much darker, and so were his eyes. The whole episode was getting me stirred up. A growl started in our kitchen, amped up a bit when the cat rotated his head in that strange slinky way cats have, and looked me right in the eye.

"What's with you?"

I twisted my head around, saw that Mama had entered the kitchen. What was with *me*? I didn't get it.

"What are you growling about?"

Growling? Me? No way! Although there was no denying that something a lot like growling was going on right in this very room. I focused my attention on giving that growling a real close listen and all at once the room went silent. Some things in this life just can't be explained.

"That's more like it," Mama said, coming closer. "What's so interesting out there? And get your paws off that window, please."

Paws on the window? Uh-oh. She was right. I got that taken care of in record time.

Mama looked out the window. "I don't see anything."

Huh? How was that possible? Possibly rising up again with my front paws on the window, I checked the street. No sign of the sporty car, the golden-haired driver, the cat. All that remained was the smell of the car's exhaust, almost lost in the bacon smell. Bacon! Why couldn't I simply have some bacon?

"Paws?" said Mama. "Window?"

Paws? Window. Meaning . . . ? Oops. I got that taken care of in record time.

"Don't tell me you're incorrigible, Mr. Birthday Present," Mama said.

That wasn't going to happen—I had no clue what she was talking about, for one thing, although the birthday present part rang a faint bell, something about how Birdie and I got together, the best day of my life except for all those that came after, right up to now. As for me and Mama, the truth was we didn't know each other very well. I kept an eye on her while she got busy with the coffee machine. Mama was wearing a loose-fitting robe, but anyone could see she was big and strong. She had light brown hair, in a ponytail at the moment, and dark brown eyes. Birdie's were blue. Also Birdie was small. They didn't look much alike. But their smells had a lot in common. I got a good feeling about Mama.

She poured coffee, started to sit at the table, paused. "Hungry, by any chance? That would be my guess."

Wow! Mama turned out to be a real good guesser. I'd have to remember that. Pretty soon I was standing over my bowl and gobbling up my morning kibble. Kibble's not bacon, but just having the bacon smell all around me some-how made the kibble taste better. That seemed like a really interesting thing to think about. I waited for a thought to come. None did.

Mama sat at the table, sipping her coffee and watching me eat.

"The size of your paws, good grief," she said. "Are you going to eat us out of house and home?"

Not sure what that meant, but I'd heard it before, many times in fact, from Grammy. For some reason hearing it now from Mama made me attack my kibble at warp speed, practically inhaling it. In fact, I did inhale some! A mis-take, but easily remedied by a quick puke, mostly right back in the bowl. And then, just in case Mama was one of those tidy types, I scarfed up all the pukey bits and licked the bowl totally clean, like the tidiest dog you'd ever want to meet. After that I sat on the floor, tail swishing back and forth, job well done. Mama and I were still getting to know each other, so my timing couldn't have been better. I was making a killer impression.

Mama's eyes narrowed, not the usual human response when it came to killer impressions, but there's a lot of variety out there in the human world. Some—Birdie, for example—sing in the shower, and others—like Grammy—do not. Birdie has a beautiful singing voice, by the way, no surprise there. What about Mama? Was she about to sing? That was my take.

Mama opened her mouth, but no singing started up. Instead, she said, "Birdie adores you. That's what counts."

Hey! Mama turned out to be pretty smart. At that moment I had an amazing thought of my own: We were one smart family! I promised myself to make an extra-special effort to hold on to that one.

Mama rubbed her eyes. The white parts were kind of reddish and the skin beneath her eyes was baggy and purple. "When are they going to solve the jet-lag problem?" she said.

The jet-lag problem? First I'd heard of it. I had problems of my own, starting with bacon and how to get it. Meanwhile, Mama was checking something on her phone. All of a sudden she sat up straight. "Is this real?" she said, her face going pale. "Wellhead price dropped three dollars a barrel overnight?"

One thing I was learning about Mama: She could be hard to follow. What did she do again? Something on the oil rigs? Off the coast of Angola, wherever that might be? All I knew was her fingernails weren't quite clean, even though I'd seen her using the kitchen sink brush on them just yesterday.

Mama took a deep breath and let it out slowly, always a

sign of a human taking charge of something inside. "What can I do?" she said. "It's good to be home, period."

Which was when Birdie came wandering into the kitchen. Just like Mama, she was rubbing her eyes, eyes the color of the big blue sky on the very nicest day.

"Hey, Mama," she said. "Were you saying something?"

Mama smiled at Birdie. "Just telling Bowser here that it's good to be home."

"He's fun to talk to, huh?" Birdie said.

"He is?"

"Bowser understands everything."

Mama laughed. She had a very nice laugh, although not quite in the class of Birdie's, meaning the best laugh you'll ever hear. Mama reached out and folded Birdie into her arms. They had a nice hug. Did I understand everything? Couldn't tell you, but after what seemed like forever I understood one thing perfectly: This hug had gone on long enough. With a hug that's gone on long enough there's only one thing to do, namely squeeze in between the huggers and break them up, which was what I did. A basic move that even puppies know.

"Jealous?" said Mama. "What other bad habits have you got?"

No time to puzzle over that, because the door to the breezeway opened and Grammy came in. Is this a good time to describe our setup here at 19 Gentilly Lane? Probably not, but when else am I going to do it?

First off, we live in St. Roch, the nicest little swampland town I know, with a bayou running right through the middle. Is that a good start? Maybe not. Maybe I should have started with Gaux Family Fish and Bait, our family business and the best family business in all of Cajun country, Cajun country being where St. Roch is, unless I've misunderstood things, always a possibility. Grammy runs Gaux Family Fish and Bait, especially the swamp tour part, and me and Birdie help out. Mama—and this gets a little tricky—is not Grammy's daughter, but the wife of Grammy's son, a cop who got killed long ago, leaving behind a medal Birdie and I look at from time to time. Kind of complicated. Should have left that part out, no doubt about it, should have left it all out and just described the house—actually two sort of small houses joined by a breezeway—which was all I'd meant to do in the first place! And now I've run out of time.

"Other bad habits?" Grammy was saying. "You name 'em."

This was interesting. Someone had bad habits? I waited to find out who, but instead Grammy went off in another direction—even better. "Breakfast, anybody? I could whip up some eggs."

8

Grammy: Where to even begin? She was pretty old, for one thing, smelled a bit like the stacks of yellowed newspapers I'd seen at the town library. Also, not very big, and kind of bony, but here's a surprise: Grammy was strong, especially her hands, which had a habit of gripping my collar very firmly at all the wrong times. Hey! Was Grammy the one with the bad habits? And she was about to spill the beans on herself?

"What's with him?" she said, suddenly turning those fierce eyes of hers on me.

"Wow!" said Mama. "His tail's practically a blur."

"It just means he's happy," said Birdie.

"Hrmff," Grammy said. "He's got plenty to be happy about. In this life we got the makers and the takers."

"Grammy!" said Birdie. "You know Bowser's not a taker!"

"Hrmff."

Mama looked from one of them to the other and blinked a couple of times, the way humans do when they're confused. Me and my kind just sort of stand there, which was what I was doing—except for my tail, which seemed to be in a real good mood about something or other.

"Tell you what," Mama said, "how about we go out for breakfast?"

"Out for breakfast?" said Birdie.

"Never heard of such a thing," said Grammy.

"On me," Mama said. "My overtime check's burning a hole in my pocket. Let's try that new food truck everyone's talking about."

"First I've heard of it," said Grammy.

Whoa! So much information! All I knew was that nothing anywhere nearby was on fire, and certainly not in Mama's pocket. I don't miss things like that.

"He's not on a leash?" Mama said.

"He really doesn't need it," Birdie said. "See how he stays right beside me?"

"Hrrmf," said Grammy.

So nice to be outside! Even nicer with every step—down Gentilly Lane, out of our neighborhood and into another one called the Dip, with the occasional washer or dryer rusting out front and a car or two up on blocks, plus clouds of bugs hovering over dampish patches in the backyards. The bacon smell grew stronger. Soon, we came to the bayou where the Lucinda Street Bridge led across to the fancy part of town. Parked by the road stood a truck painted all sorts of colors, with one side panel open and a chimney pipe poking out the top. And out of that chimney poured the smell of bacon like I'd never smelled it before!

A sweaty man with an apron around his middle and a do-rag on his head looked over the countertop from inside.

"Hey, there, Miz Gaux," he said. "And Miz Gaux the younger. And Birdie. What can I do you for?"

"Wally Tebbets?" Grammy said.

"At your service, ma'am."

"Now you've got a food truck?"

"Best food truck in Acadiana," Wally Tebbets said. He had bacon on his breath! What a cool dude! "Possibly the whole state of Louisiana."

"What happened to your lube job joint?" Grammy said.

"I kind of . . . evolved," said Wally.

"Uh-huh," Grammy said. "Where'd you learn how to cook?"

"In the blood, ma'am. Us Tebbets been cookin' since the world began."

"We'll be the judge of that," said Grammy. "What's the best thing on your menu?"

"Blue crab and pepper po'boy, hands down."

Grammy nodded. "I'll chance it."

"Make that two," Mama said.

"Three," said Birdie.

Wally Tebbets got to work. A kid popped up beside him, a real skinny kid with a dark tan, a Mohawk haircut, and an earring in one ear.

"Hey, Birdie," he said.

"Hey, Junior."

"School's in two weeks."

"Don't I know it."

"Maybe a hurricane will come," Junior said.

Wally Tebbets gave him a smack, not hard. "Watch your mouth."

Junior ducked from sight, then popped out a door at the back of the truck. He motioned for Birdie. She took maybe a half step in his direction. So did I. Junior was an unknown quantity. I was security.

Junior lowered his voice. "Birdie?"

"Yeah?"

"Can you sing?"

"Sing?"

"Like, you know." Then from out of Junior's mouth came a strange kind of yowl. "Down by the river, I shot my baby."

"You call that singing?"

"I'm not a singer. I'm a drummer." With his open hands, Junior did some fast pounding on the side of the food truck.

"Knock it off," yelled Wally from inside.

"But I need a singer," Junior said. "I'm starting a band— Junior Tidbit and His All-Stars."

"Junior Tidbit?"

"Cool, huh?"

"No."

"We can always change it," Junior said. "But I gotta have a singer. Sing."

"Like what?"

"Try that one I just did—*Down by the River.*"

"This is stupid, Junior."

Junior got down on one knee. I considered bowling him over, held back for the moment.

"For heaven's sake," Birdie said. Then she took a breath and started to sing. "Down by the river, I shot my baby."

Silence fell all around us. Had I ever heard anything so beautiful? Yes, every time Birdie sang in the shower. But it seemed to be new to everyone else: They were all staring at Birdie, their eyebrows raised way up.

"You got the job," Junior said.

"No, thanks," said Birdie.

Not long after that, Wally Tebbets handed out the po'boys and all of us Gaux, excepting me, were happily chowing down. Wally glanced my way. "What about the pooch?"

"What about him?" said Grammy.

"Think he's hungry?"

"He's just been fed," Mama said.

Wally shrugged. "Happen to have some leftover bacon that got burned."

And I don't remember anything after that until we were almost back home. Burned bacon turned out to be the very best bacon out there. That was my takeaway. I was still going over the wonder of it when 19 Gentilly Lane came into view.

"Whoa!" Grammy said. "Did somebody leave the door open?"

"Not me," Mama said.

"Or me," said Birdie.

And not me, either. But the breezeway door to our side of the house—meaning mine, Birdie's, and Mama's—was open for sure, and not just open but hanging at a funny angle. A moment after that, we were all running, even Grammy.

two

HOW AMAZING THAT HUMANS CAN actually run without falling flat on their faces! Only two legs—can you imagine? So what if they don't run fast! Which was why I was first to the door at our place at 19 Gentilly Lane—first by plenty. And I wasn't even running my fastest, not nearly, my stomach being a little too full for that sort of effort.

The door hung crooked from the top hinge; the wood splintered right off the bottom one. My mood, which had been sky-high, began to change. Who was in charge of security at 19 Gentilly Lane? Me! So what was our door doing like this? I barked one of my short, sharp barks, just getting my feelings out there. Then came a surprise, and not a good one: I picked up the scent of cat. Cat scent is one of the strongest scents out there, impossible to miss. A cat had been—and maybe still was, at this very moment— inside our house? Don't there have to be some limits in this life? The next thing I knew I was running from room to room, head down, tail up, on high alert.

First, the kitchen. Nothing looked different from when we'd left. The differences were all about smell. We had the smell of cat, and also the smell of a man I'd never smelled before. I barked another short bark, sharper than the one before. The mannish part of the man scent was a bit on the faint side, mostly overwhelmed by the powerful smell of one of those aftershaves some dudes splash on, and this particular dude had clearly splashed on plenty. The whole house smelled like limeade, a drink Birdie likes on hot days but does nothing for me.

Second, down the hall. Mama's door was closed so I hurried to our room, meaning mine and Birdie's, where the door stood open. A beautiful room, by the way, walls the color of the summer, with a puffy cloud here and there and even a rainbow, but the point was nothing had changed. Our room was just as we'd left it, bed unmade, clothes all over the floor, pretty much perfect. Had the man and the cat even gone inside? I didn't think so. Cat scent and limeade scent didn't extend more than a step or two across the threshold.

I checked the bathroom, lapped up a quick sip of water from the toilet, and doubled back up the hall, arriving at Mama's room just as she got there and opened the door.

"Oh my god," she said, putting her hand to her chest and stepping back. I pushed in front of her and looked in. Mama's room was a total wreck, everything upside down, all the drawers pulled out and dumped, papers scattered across the floor, the bed frame up on its side and the mattress sliced right through. All the paintings and photos had been knocked off the wall. The only thing remaining in place was Mama's hard hat, on a hook by the closet door. As for cat smell and limeade smell: We had plenty of both. Intruders! Intruders had come into our home and made a mess of Mama's room. I barked again, this time sharp enough to scare the pants off any intruder. But too late! Too late: That made me bark again, the sharpest bark ever. It even scared me a bit.

Birdie and Grammy pressed in behind us. Birdie caught her breath. Poor kid. I turned and pressed against her. Grammy said, "Someone's gonna pay." Mama moved into the room. She bent down and picked up one of the framed photos. Birdie had shown me this particular photo more than once. In it Mama—a slightly smoother-skinned Mama—stood beside a big man in a uniform, their arms around each other and smiles on their faces; not the biggest smiles, but real happy ones. The big man in the uniform was Birdie's dad, killed a long time ago, the details escaping me. Wait! Here was one: Birdie had a lone single memory of her dad, from when she'd been very little. He'd tied the laces of her shoes—tiny blue shoes with silver stars on them—and said, "No loose ends, Birdie."

But back to the photo. I saw that its cardboard backing

had been ripped away. Mama was examining that when the frame came apart in her hands. How white her face was! And Birdie's, too. I barked a bark that shook the house.

"I hear you," Grammy said. "Don't no one touch another darn thing. I'm calling the cops."

"Hmm," said Sheriff Cannon.

"Well, well," said Officer Perkins in his deep, rumbly voice.

They looked down at what had happened to Mama's room, both of them tall in their khaki uniforms, although Officer Perkins was quite a bit broader. We'd gotten to know Sheriff Cannon and Officer Perkins almost too well, me and Birdie, during a sort of adventure we'd had earlier in the summer. Plus Sheriff Cannon was the father of Birdie's friend Rory, and the Cannons lived with a very small and very noisy member of my tribe, name of Sugarplum. Surprisingly sharp-toothed. I'll leave it at that.

The sheriff and Perkins rocked back and forth in their huge black shoes and Perkins said, "Well, well," again.

"*Well, well* won't get it done," Grammy said, standing behind them in the hall.

The sheriff and Perkins turned to her. From the expression on their faces you might have thought these two big

18

guys with guns on their hips were afraid of Grammy. This was no surprise to me. I knew Grammy.

"Don't want to rush in, ma'am," the sheriff said. "Can't risk contaminating the evidence."

Grammy, so small compared to these men, but with her posture so straight, somehow seemed to take up more space than they did. "Then how about snapping crime scene photos for starters? Get the show on the road."

The sheriff's face, all about hard features—square chin, big nose, bushy eyebrows—got harder. He tried staring down at Grammy. That didn't seem to have any effect on her. She stared right back, those washed-out blue eyes unblinking. The sheriff sighed and pointed at Perkins. Perkins took out a camera and clicked away. He hummed in a deep, soft voice, like he was enjoying himself. "Framed that one real nice," he muttered.

The sheriff turned to Mama. "You all right?"

Mama nodded.

"Glass of water?"

"I'm fine."

The sheriff gave her a longish look and finally nodded. "Anything missing?" he said.

"Nothing so far," Mama said. "I haven't had time to really look."

"What about valuables?"

"There's just my jewelry."

The sheriff gazed into the room. "See any of it?"

Mama scanned the mess from one side to the other. "There," she said. "By the mattress."

The sheriff snapped on thin plastic gloves, went into the room, returned with a small black pouch, just plain leather, nothing fancy. He opened it and Mama checked inside. She shook her head. "All here," she said.

"Do you keep any cash in the room?" the sheriff said.

"No."

He glanced around, motioned to what looked like a big gold coin lying in the fold of a curtain that had been ripped off its rod. "What's that?"

Mama moved into the room. Perkins stopped humming and extended his arm to block her, but Mama didn't seem to notice and brushed right by him. She crouched down and folded up the big gold coin in both hands. Very quietly, Birdie said, "That's the medal of honor the New Orleans police department gave my dad after . . . after."

"Ah," said the sheriff, also very quietly.

Mama started to rise, then paused. She reached into a fold in the fallen curtain, picked up a shred of what looked like blue velvet, then another, and another. "They—they sliced up the box," she said, in the kind of low tone humans sometimes use when talking to themselves.

"The box?" said the sheriff.

Mama turned to him and blinked. "The presentation box the medal came in. It's cut to ribbons. But they didn't take the medal."

"Was anything else in there?" the sheriff said. "Tucked in the lining, maybe?"

"Like what?"

"I don't know. Something valuable."

Mama shook her head.

"Why would they slice up the box?" the sheriff said.

"Why any of this?" said Mama.

Birdie reached out and took Mama's hand. I pressed up against Birdie again, perhaps a little too hard, although Mama caught her before she fell. So, things could have been worse, in my opinion. They would have been even better if we lost the cat smell and the limeade smell, but they were everywhere in Mama's room. I waited for someone to mention it. No one did.

"Get someone up here to canvass the neighbors while you dust for prints," the sheriff said.

"Ten-four," said Perkins.

Not long after that we had yellow tape barring the way into Mama's bedroom—in our own house!—and were sitting with the sheriff under the umbrella in our little backyard, the humans in our mismatched collection of plastic chairs and me on the ground. I could hear Perkins humming inside the house, and also a faraway boat horn. Normally that sound would have put me in the mood for a boat ride—nothing like a boat ride, and we had a couple of nice boats down at Gaux Family Fish and Bait. But now I wasn't in the mood for a boat ride. I could tell by how my tail was just lying there on the ground, like a sad old thing. Who was in charge of security at 19 Gentilly Lane? Me.

The sheriff took out a notebook. "Do you have any enemies you know of?" he asked Mama.

Mama shook her head. She had two faint vertical lines on her forehead, not so faint today.

"I got enemies," Grammy said. "By the boatload."

Boatload? Had I heard right? I moved closer to Grammy, maybe my best chance when it came to a boat ride anytime soon.

The sheriff turned to her. "Maybe we'll get to that," he said. "But your part of the house wasn't even entered. All the damage happened in your daughter-in-law's room."

"So?" said Grammy. "Ever heard of thinking outside the box?"

"In my experience, ma'am, most criminals never get outside the box."

Grammy thought about that. I expected her to say "Hrrmf." She did not. That made me a bit uneasy. Don't know about you, but when I'm uneasy, tearing up a patch of grass with my paws tends to do wonders for my mood. I hadn't even gotten started, not properly, before I felt Birdie's hand on my collar, not gripping hard, just there.

The sheriff turned back to Mama. "I understand you recently returned from a job?"

Mama nodded.

"In the oil business, if I remember," the sheriff said.

"I'm an engineer with Marine Drilling, out of Houston. We were doing some retooling on a rig off Angola."

"That's in Africa?"

"Yes."

"Sounds kind of adventurous."

"It's really not," Mama said.

One of my habits is to keep an eye out for Birdie, which was how come I didn't miss the look on her face while she watched Mama explaining what was or wasn't adventurous, rather confusing from where I sat. That look, kind of shining, said Mama was just aces in her book.

"What about your coworkers?" Sheriff Cannon said.

"What about them?"

"Any problems? Rivalries, maybe? You getting a promotion someone else was angling for? Just some ordinary personal conflict, what with working at such close quarters and all?"

"Nothing like that," Mama said. "These are good jobs, Sheriff, and we all know it. No one wants to jeopardize that paycheck."

"Makes sense." The sheriff wrote in his notebook, flipped to a new page. A blank page, which I could see from where I was, but he kept gazing at it when he said, "I heard your husband lecture once at the police academy. All about the importance of having a theory of the case. I never forgot it." He looked up. Mama's eyes glistened. Grammy's were hard and dry. Birdie's, glued to the sheriff's face, were just plain watchful. A heavy sort of silence lowered itself on our backyard. The boat horn blew again, farther away now, almost out of my hearing.

"What did he say?" Birdie said.

"Too much to go into now," the sheriff said. "But you might want to drop in on Rory. He's down in the dumps."

"Baseball?" Birdie said.

"Oh-for-fifty-three, although why coaches keep batting averages for eleven-year-old kids is beyond me." He gave his head a quick shake. I do something similar with my whole body. Hey! The sheriff and I were buddies! "But," he went on, "here's something else your . . . your dad said that day: 'You warm up cold cases by caring about the survivors.'"

"The survivors?" Birdie said, her voice suddenly a bit faint.

"I think he was talking about murder, specifically," the sheriff said. "The survivors are those left behind—the families, loved ones, friends of the victim."

Birdie nodded, just a slight little nod.

"Didn't realize it at the time," the sheriff went on, "but that was when I first got a handle on what I was actually supposed to do in this career."

"Words," Grammy said. "Just words."

The sheriff's face got red. "What are you saying?" he said, his voice sharpening.

Grammy's voice sharpened, too. "I'm saying they'll never find out who killed my boy. I call down to New Orleans every year on the anniversary, and what do I get? Words." She made a fist, actually shook it at the sheriff. "Action! They teach you anything about action at that academy of yours? You all have forgotten how to get things done."

The sheriff got even redder, opened his mouth like he was about to say something real angry, but just then Perkins appeared on the breezeway and came toward us, a phone in his hand. Perkins seemed to have spilled some sort of white powder all over himself, which I found kind of scary, so I'm not sure if I caught all the details of what came next.

"Anything from the neighbors?" the sheriff said.

"Nobody saw nor heard nothin'," said Perkins. "And I'm all done inside. But, Boss? Report coming in of a break-in that sounds a lot like this one, over on Huey Street—number two hundred three."

The sheriff rose. "Who lives there?"

"Family name of Richelieu," Perkins said.

The sheriff nodded. "Didn't they sell some resort down in Biloxi, move here a couple years ago?" He turned to Mama. "Know the Richelieus on Huey Street?"

"Never heard of them," Mama said. "Does this mean . . . ?"

"Too soon to say anything on that score," said the sheriff. And a moment or two later he and Perkins were gone. I heard their cruiser peeling away out front. They hit the siren.

"Just words," said Grammy.

three

WE GOT TO WORK CLEANING UP
Mama's room. I helped out a lot in the
beginning, but the beginning didn't last
very long for some reason, and soon after that Birdie and I
got sent down to check on things at the store. I kept my
eye out for strangers the whole way, but saw none. What
if the intruders came back? They would pay, as Grammy
had said. Whoa! Did I have something in common with
Grammy? I got rid of that thought immediately.

Gaux Family Fish and Bait backs right onto the bayou,
where we've got a dock for tying up our boats—*Bayou Girl*
for fishing, and the flat-bottomed aluminum pirogue for
swamp tours. The store is low and yellow, with a wrap-
around porch where buoys and nets hang from one end to
the other. The best thing is the sign on the roof. It's in the
shape of a big fish! "Sends a message," Grammy says, and
I knew if I just paid attention that one day I'd find out
what it was.

We went inside. Snoozy LaChance was in charge. Hey!
He was awake, and not only that, he had a customer.

". . . I got a sixth sense for where the fish are holin' up,"
he was telling her. "Nothin' to be vain about. Call it a gift,
kinda like Einstein and math."

The woman, on the youngish side, had hair cut short on
one side and long on the other, the short side being dark
and the long side green. She also wore a lot of rings in her
ears. That always made my own ears kind of buzzy, hard
to explain why. I gave them a sideways swipe or two with
my paws, felt better. Meanwhile, the woman was pointing
at Snoozy's arm. He wore a sleeveless T-shirt, revealing
lots of tattoos.

"All your tats are fish?" the woman said.

"Just part of the package," said Snoozy. "Check it out—
all the local varieties and then some, like a walkin'
guidebook. Right arm is freshwater. Here's carp, catfish,
bream, largemouth, striped, and over on the left we got
saltwater: 'cuda, marlin, swordfish, tunny. You name it, I
got it. Back of the elbow's red snapper. Kind of hard to
see." Snoozy twisted his arm around in a way that looked
painful.

"Cool," said the woman.

"So how's about I book you for a full day on *Bayou
Girl*?" Snoozy said.

"I'll think about it."

"There's always the half day. Costs half."

"I'll think about it."

"For half the time of your first think?" said Snoozy. He burst out laughing, like something really funny had just happened. A small—although far from tiny—particle of food flew out of his mouth, landed on the floor not far from me. I scarfed it up. Sausage. I have all the luck in the world.

When I got done with that I saw that the customer was on her way out of the store, moving quite quickly—although she darted one glance back at Snoozy's mouth. Around then was when Snoozy, still chuckling softly to himself, noticed us.

"Oh, hi, Birdie."

I'm sure he noticed me, too, just forgot to mention it. Snoozy was one of the best forgetters you'd ever want to meet.

"Hey, Snoozy. How's it goin'?"

"Cookin' with gas. You can tell your grammy I got one on the line."

Gas? We'd had problems with Snoozy and gas in the past, flames erupting right on the surface of the bayou being a sight that's hard to forget. But I smelled no gas, and that's not the kind of thing I miss.

"What are you talking about?" Birdie said, a sure sign that she and I were pretty much thinking as one. What a team! With her beauty and my brains, unless I was mixing that up somehow—and also my beauty, too, what with people always saying what a handsome dude I was and giving me nice pats—there was no stopping us.

Snoozy pointed with his chin at the door. "Deep pockets."

"Huh?"

"Customer who just left. Comes from money, clear as day."

"How do you know that?"

Snoozy rubbed the side of his nose. Right away I wanted to do the very same thing. Don't tell me I was also thinking as one with Snoozy!

"What's wrong with your nose?" Birdie said.

"My nose? Nada. Unless there's a booger I'm not aware of. Happens to the best of us." He stuck his finger in his nose, explored around. That was the first time in my life I've ever wished for a finger of my own! "Nope," said Snoozy. "All clear."

Birdie was watching him with eyes that somehow reminded me of Grammy's, even though Grammy's eyes are all washed out and Birdie's are so bright and full of color. I wouldn't want that look turned on me, even though it was Birdie.

"Did you get her name?" she said.

"Who you referencin'?" said Snoozy. And then he yawned, a huge yawn that seemed to come out of nowhere, taking him by surprise. "My goodness," he said, glancing at an old couch out on the porch, an old couch where Grammy had told him she'd better not find him ever again.

"The woman with the deep pockets." Birdie gestured out the window to the parking lot, where the woman was hopping onto a dusty and dented motorcycle.

"Nope," said Snoozy. "But she got ours, so we're hunky-dory."

"Ours?"

"More like yours, I guess."

"Mine?"

"Not the Birdie part. She wanted to know who the owners were."

"It's right on the sign—Gaux Family Fish and Bait."

"Exactly what I told her."

"And?"

"And she said she was just making sure it was up to date."

"I wonder why," Birdie said. She gazed out the window. The young woman was speeding off on the motorcycle, her hair—the long, greenish part—streaming in the wind. A small dust cloud hung over the parking lot, sparkling with sunshine. I felt good about everything.

"Don't ask me," said Snoozy, yawning again. He checked his watch. "My, my—practically lunchtime already. Mind covering for me?"

"It's not even eleven o'clock," Birdie said.

"Just going by what my stomach is telling me," Snoozy said. "It's sayin' lunchtime, Snoozy boy."

Hey! My stomach was saying the same thing, except for the Snoozy boy part. Next maybe Birdie would say, "Let's all break for lunch."

But she did not. Instead, she said, "Not now, Snoozy. Something's come up."

"Anything I need to know about?"

She gave him another one of those hard looks. Then came a surprise: Her eyes filled with tears.

"Hey!" Snoozy said. "What did I say?"

Birdie blinked the tears away real quick, only one getting loose and rolling down her cheek. Human tears were salty, a fact I'd proved to myself in the past and would prove again if this single loose tear would only trickle off Birdie's chin and fall to the floor. Birdie wiped it off on the back of her hand before that could happen.

"It's not you, Snoozy. We . . . we had a break-in."

"Whoa!" Snoozy glanced around kind of wildly. "We did? I don't see nothin' missin'. 'Ceptin' maybe that trollin' combo from that German company." He hurried out from behind the counter, walked over to a display cabinet by the door. "Nope, here it is." He bent down, picked up a fishing rod, placed it on top of the cabinet. "Musta forgotten to—"

"Snoozy! I don't mean here."

"Whew."

"It was at home."

"Oh. That's good. I mean, uh . . ."

"Doesn't matter." Birdie started telling Snoozy the story of the break-in, but in such a speedy jumble that I got lost right from the get-go, even though I knew the whole thing. So I was glad when the door to Gaux Family Fish and Bait flew open and our pal Nola Claymore came running in.

"Birdie! Is it true?"

Birdie nodded. Nola rushed over and gave her a tight hug. She was our pal but already in place as Birdie's best friend before I came along, so I let this hug go on for a very long time. An unbearably long time, but here's a chance to describe Nola, not an easy thing to do, except for her smell, which was lemony with hints of honey, totally nice although not in Birdie's class. But who on earth could be? Nola was a lot taller than Birdie, had skin the color of coffee with lots of cream stirred in, the way Grammy liked it, and was an excellent patter and scratcher between the ears. That's all you need to know. I pushed between them in my most polite way.

"Oh, Bowser," Birdie said, which I took to mean she'd missed me and was happy I was back. Nola laughed and gave me a pat, first-rate as usual but not long enough. Then Birdie backed up and started in again on the whole break-in story, losing me once more! Wow! How can you explain something like that? Impossible! Meanwhile, Nola was saying, "The Richelieus over on Huey Street?"

"Yeah," said Birdie. "You know them?"

"Customers of the store," Nola said, meaning not our shop, Gaux Family Fish and Bait, but Claymore's General Store in the center of town, where they sold a certain kind of dog biscuit I always had time for. Like now, at this very moment! No biscuits available, of course. Nola did have gum in her pocket, strawberry flavor. Gum does nothing for me. I've had unpleasant experiences with gum once or twice or even more, always ending up with a big blob caught up in the roof of my mouth, followed by gagging and choking and a promise to myself never to let it happen again.

"How come Bowser's sniffing at your pocket?" Birdie said.

"No idea. All that's in there is some gum."

"He's not allowed gum."

I wasn't? Why not? But if Birdie said no gum, then that was that. I backed away, made myself pretty much unnoticeable.

"Why's he doing that?" Nola said.

"Doing what?" said Birdie.

"Just staring at the wall with his tongue hanging out."

"He does that sometimes."

"Yeah," said Snoozy, "when he's making plans."

"Plans?" said Birdie.

"What plans?" said Nola.

I watched all this, kind of over my shoulder, which I can do without turning my head, maybe unlike you.

Snoozy shrugged. "Doggy-type plans."

"Like?" said Birdie and Nola together.

Snoozy shrugged again and said nothing. Too bad! I wanted to hear some doggy-type plans in the worst way. But no luck. Next thing I knew we were on our way out the door—me, Birdie, Nola—and Snoozy was calling after us. "Wouldn't mind a little snack if you're coming back soon."

". . . never heard of Preston Richelieu?" Nola was saying as we walked through our neighborhood and headed up a gentle rise—all the rises in these parts being gentle, with hardly anything you'd call a hill anywhere in sight, except for the banks of the levee—that took us into North St. Roch, one of the nicest parts of town. Was it nice because the houses here were bigger and more spaced out, or on account of the septic tank smells being stronger? I had no clue.

"Nope," said Birdie.

"Football star at the high school."

"Go, Hornets."

"*Woo-woo*," Nola said. "He's been hanging out with Solange lately." Solange being Nola's sister, if I was remembering right, but my mind was elsewhere, namely on hornets. I listened my hardest and heard none. That didn't stop the tip of my nose from getting an unpleasant feeling. The tip of my nose knew about hornets, knew way too much.

"Ah," Birdie said. "Solange."

"The one and only," said Nola.

"How's she doing in summer school?" Birdie said.

"That's where she got to know Preston."

"I meant with her classes."

"Who knows? She's driving my mom to distraction. Her latest is that she's too smart for school."

"On account of that IQ test your mom had her take?"

"One thirty-five. Puts her in the top something or other in the whole country. Meanwhile, if she doesn't shape up she'll be repeating tenth grade."

"Wow," Birdie said. After that came a long silence. We turned down a street lined by tall, shady trees. Tree shadows darkened Birdie's face. "School."

"You can say that again," said Nola, but Birdie did not. Nola pointed to a big house with a nice green lawn that looked like a putting green. "The Richelieus' place." A police cruiser was parked out front. All of a sudden I seemed to be getting a message from that lawn: Dig, Bowser. Was that a good idea? I went back and forth on that question, still hadn't decided when we came to the house. The front door opened and Sheriff Cannon stepped out, putting on his hat.

"Birdie?" he said. "Nola? What are you doing here?"

"Um," Birdie said. "Is this where the other break-in happened?"

"So?"

By that time, the sheriff had reached us. He peered down at Birdie with an expression that didn't seem too friendly. Birdie looked very small next to the sheriff. At times like these, she has a way of standing very straight and not blinking. You had to love Birdie, and everyone did. And if not everyone, there was always me.

"So we were curious," Birdie said.

"About what?"

Birdie thought. Her face turned a bit pink. Then Nola said, "About whether there were similarities."

"Similarities?" said the sheriff.

"Yeah," said Birdie. She gave her head a quick and sort of fierce little shake and the pinkness vanished from her face. "Similarities in the MO."

There was a pause. Was the sheriff trying not to smile? I got that feeling, just from a tiny glint in his eyes. "What's MO?"

"Modus something or other."

"Been watching too many cops shows?" the sheriff said. "Modus operandi—means how something is done."

"Like if the bad guy always gets in by busting the lock," Birdie said.

"Correct," said the sheriff. "And exactly that—busting the lock—has happened in these two break-ins. So the answer is yes, the MOs look pretty similar for now, except that certain items are missing in this case."

"What kind of items?" Birdie said.

The sheriff got in the cruiser. "That's not public information yet. How about you kids go play somewhere?" He drove off.

"Play somewhere?" Nola said.

Birdie started to laugh, then got sidetracked by a face that appeared in an upstairs window of the Richelieus' house. "Who's that?" she said, lowering her voice.

Nola looked up. "Preston," she said, meeting his gaze. Preston made a gun shape with his hand and pulled the trigger.

four

WHAT A JERK," BIRDIE SAID.

"Didn't I mention that already?" said Nola.

Preston was still in the window, a big grin on his face. Most human smiles are happy and just seeing them gives you a good feeling. Others send a nasty message. Preston's was of that kind. It got me riled up a bit. Not much I could do about it, not with Preston up there and me down here. I could growl at him, of course, or bark, or . . .

A very pleasant idea hit me from out of the blue. Maybe it would have hit you, too, if you'd been in my position. If so, the next thing you'd have done would have been to trot in a leisurely way across the Richelieus' lovely soft lawn, over to a flowering bush near the house. A big bush with lots of flowers in all kinds of colors, really a thing of beauty. Then you'd have raised your leg and marked that beautiful flowering bush, marked it to the best of your ability, meaning up, down, sideways, and even inside out—one of my very best techniques, which often ends with me in a tangle, but this time did not.

"Uh-oh," Nola said.

"Bowser!" said Birdie, in a kind of whispered shout. I didn't recall hearing a whispered shout from her anytime in the past. She must have been especially pleased with me. That was my takeaway. I got back to work and was just about done when the Richelieus' front door flew open.

Out stomped a rather large man who seemed to be in the middle of getting dressed. He wore dark pants and an unbuttoned, untucked white shirt—and one shoe. He had the other shoe—of the type called a tassel loafer, I believe; those tassels an interest of mine going way back— in his hand.

"What is going on out here?"

What a booming voice he had! And his face, reddish to begin with, was getting redder, and fast. Did we have a problem of some sort? None that I could think of.

"G'wan," he said, quite possibly glaring my direction. "Git! Git or else, you ugly cur."

Ugly cur? Couldn't be me. And even if it was, calling a sudden halt to my activity at the moment just wasn't in the cards. Some things when started have to be seen through to the end, which I'm sure he'd understand if he only paused to—

"You deaf?" The man had real dark and heavy eyebrows that were all bunched up like they had a temper of their own. Then his whole body seemed to bunch

and he flung that tassel loafer at me, whipped it rea

It spun through the air with a sizzling sound.

"Hey!" Birdie said.

But there was nothing to worry about. Ol' Bowser snagged the tassel loafer clean out of the sky in one easy motion. Snap! Just like that! Woke me up, I can tell you. I'd never felt so wide awake in my whole life.

"Bowser! Whoa!"

Nothing to worry about! If the rather large gentleman was in the mood to play some fetch, he'd found the right buddy, namely me. I was all done with my marking responsibilities: He had my full attention! I took off across the putting green lawn in a zigzag pattern, making sharp cuts, clumps of turf flying high, the wonderful feeling of high-quality leather tassels between my teeth. They tasted superb! Which you know already if you're living life to the max.

"BOWSER!"

And suddenly Birdie had me by the collar. Sort of. Where had she come from? We tumbled together across the lawn, coming to rest at the bottom of the front step of the Richelieus' house, which looked even bigger from that angle.

Three people now stood outside the door. First, the rather large man wearing one shoe. Second, Preston, who was

flab. He wore a sleeveless T-shirt
opping un-Snoozy-like muscles in
an dressed in an office-job-type
for one eye that had no makeup.
unfriendly. The other, all made
dark and also unfriendly.

om," said Birdie, scrambling to her feet, hand still on
my collar. I scrambled up, too, got ready for . . . for more
fetch? That was what I wanted. Did anyone else want anything different? If so, I couldn't think what.

Nola came over. "Hello, Preston," she said.

"Huh?" said Preston. He had eyebrows like the rather
large gentleman, maybe not quite so bushy but just as . . .
as pushy! Wow! All at once my mind was at the very top of
its game.

"Nola Claymore," Nola said. "Solange's sister."

"Uh," said Preston.

"Claymore of Claymore's General Store?" said the rather
large gentleman.

"That's right," Nola said.

"Thought I recognized you," said the woman.

"Hi, Mrs. Richelieu," Nola said. She turned to the rather
large gentleman and nodded. "Mr. Richelieu."

"Never mind all the pleasantries," Mr. Richelieu said. "I
want my shoe and I want it now."

42

"Bowser?" Birdie said. "Be good."

"Who are you?" said Mr. Richelieu.

"Birdie."

"Birdie who?" said Mrs. Richelieu.

"Gaux."

"Gaux?" said Mrs. Richelieu, like she wasn't happy to hear it. She exchanged a look with Mr. Richelieu, one of those meaningful human looks, totally over my head.

"Yeah," Birdie said, standing tall in that lovely way she had. And as a bonus, besides the lovely part, she maybe got distracted a little bit, and let go of my collar.

Be good. Those were my marching orders, meaning I had to be good now, my very best. And what's the very best thing I do? So many good ones, really, but the very best? Had to be running! I love everything about running—the whistle of the wind, the way my ears lie back, the pounding of my heart. Therefore, being good meant running my very fastest, didn't it? I couldn't come up with any other conclusion in the time I devoted to the problem, which was not a lot, because . . . because *ZOOM!*

"BOWSER!"

Oh, how wonderful it is to know you're being good! I was in heaven, if that's a place where your paws hardly touch the ground. I tore across the lawn, straight through what might have been a flower bed—hard to tell above certain speeds—and then made a sharp turn and the next thing I knew I was in the backyard, a huge fenced-in back yard with a nice big pool. I dove in—

"BOWSER!"

—enjoyed the very briefest of swims, scrambled up to the pool deck, gave myself a good shake, water flying every-where, even making my own rainbow!—

"SIT! SIT DOWN THIS SECOND!"

—and then vaulted high over—*sitting? Something about sitting?*—a poolside table, or perhaps not quite as high as all that, because my trailing paw somehow caught an object and I landed with it wrapped around my leg. Glancing back, I saw that the object was a big, floppy purse and what was wrapped around my leg was actually the strap. A hand came out of nowhere and grabbed my collar good and hard.

I looked up. Birdie looked down. "Bowser," she said in a low voice. "What got into you?"

Something in me? I had no clue. And I wanted badly to help: Birdie didn't look happy and I hate seeing that. Still holding my collar in a—what's the expression? Death grip?—Birdie got me untangled from the purse, which she placed back up on the table and—

Oops. Not quite, the purse tipped sideways and spilled out a string of pearls. A long string of big, fat pearls, quite beautiful. I asked myself the obvious question: What would they be like to chew on? But I never found out, because Birdie scooped up the string of pearls, dropped them in the purse, and set the purse carefully on the table, right side up. Just then, the Richelieus and Nola came running into the backyard, Preston in the lead, followed by Nola and Mrs. Richelieu, with Mr. Richelieu hobbling a bit—maybe on account of the fact that he seemed to be missing one shoe—a distant last.

And here was something amazing. That missing shoe? I still had it in my mouth! Very gently, Birdie pried the shoe—a tassel loafer, if I remembered right—out from between my teeth, me hardly resisting at all, and handed what was left of it, now smelling strongly of swimming pool, over to Mr. Richelieu. He stared at it in a puzzled way, like he'd never seen a shoe before.

"Um," said Birdie, "ah, it's just that we got broken into, too, and . . . uh—"

"And what?" said Mrs. Richelieu, grabbing the purse and slinging the strap over her shoulder.

"And," said Nola, "we . . . we wanted to compare notes."

"Compare notes?" Mrs. Richelieu said.

"Yeah," said Birdie. "See if there are similarities, maybe develop a theory of the case."

"Theory of the case?" said Mrs. Richelieu.

"What is she even talking about?" said Preston.

"Preston?" said Mrs. Richelieu.

"That's my name," Preston said.

"Zip it," said Mr. Richelieu. "Miranda and I will handle this."

Miranda—which had to be Mrs. Richelieu's first name—shot Mr. Richelieu an annoyed look. I kept my own gaze on her made-up eye, which turned out to be less scary than the unmade-up one. She turned back to Birdie.

"Well?" she said. "Go on."

"Theory of the case?" Birdie said. "I guess it's all about understanding who did what and why."

"It was your dad's idea, right, Birdie?" said Nola.

"Maybe not his own original idea, but he believed in it."

"Birdie's dad was a hero," Nola said.

"Oh?" said Miranda Richelieu.

"He was a police detective," Birdie said. "Maybe you knew him."

"Certainly not," said Miranda, backing up a step.

"No way," said Mr. Richelieu. "How could we ever—"

Miranda cut him off. "Merv? I'll handle this." She turned to Birdie, gave her a smile. Actually, it was more like just showing teeth. "Birdie, is it?"

"Yes, ma'am."

"I think it would be best if you removed the dog before he does any more damage."

Dog? Damage? What was that all about? Don't ask me.

■ ■ ■

"Thanks," said Birdie, when we were out on the street.

"What for?" said Nola.

"Bailing me out."

"I didn't."

"You did—the comparing notes thing."

Nola shrugged. "We're a team."

I liked Nola, but she'd gotten that wrong. Birdie and I were the team. Anyone can make a mistake, and I'm the forgiving type. I gave Nola a friendly bump on the back of her leg, a bump of the no-harm-done kind.

"Ouch," said Nola, stumbling a bit, perhaps, but not actually going flat down on the sidewalk. She could be funny sometimes.

When we got back home, Dr. Rajatawan was just on his way out. "Hi, Birdie," he said. "Hey there, Bowser."

I was a big fan of Dr. Rajatawan. Humans often smell of what they've been eating, a fun fact you may not know. Today, for example, Dr. Rajatawan smelled of fried chicken. Hard to top that.

"Dr. Rajatawan?" Birdie said. "Is something wrong?" How could anything be wrong with fried chicken in the breeze? I wasn't following this at all.

"Just checking up on your grandmother," Dr. Rajatawan said.

"But I thought it was just dehydration," said Birdie. Had I heard about that before? I kind of remembered Grammy fainting in the yard a while back, not far from where I was at the moment. I went over and sniffed at the spot, smelled a worm not far below the surface.

"True as far as it goes," Dr. Rajatawan said. "She's in excellent shape, considering."

"Considering her age?" said Birdie.

Dr. Rajatawan paused. "That's one way to put it."

Tiny wrinkles appeared on Birdie's forehead, normally the smoothest in town. "Is there something else wrong with her? Besides being old?"

"That's usually the case when it comes to—" Dr. Rajatawan stopped himself, began again. "Nothing for you to be worried about, Birdie."

"But . . . but you're getting me worried."

"I'm very sorry—not my intention at all." Dr. Rajatawan glanced at the house. "But maybe you could be a help."

"Me? How?"

"I sense some resistance when it comes to her medications."

"All those pills?" Birdie said. "Grammy hates them."

"Just as I feared," said Dr. Rajatawan. "That's what my visit was mostly about—stressing the importance of taking the exact right pills at the exact right times. I got the feeling she wasn't quite as . . . receptive as I'd hoped."

"What did she do?"

"Let's just say it's a good thing your mom's here," Dr. Rajatawan said. "But maybe in the future if you could just encourage your grandmother, maybe . . ." His eyes brightened the way human eyes do when a big idea comes along. ". . . maybe make a game of it!"

"Make a game of what?" Birdie said.

"Of taking the pills," Dr. Rajatawan said. "How good at games we are!"

"We?"

"Why, we Americans, of course. This is one of the most amazing things I've learned since coming to this country. We know games! So I'm sure you'll think of something."

"Um," said Birdie.

Dr. Rajatawan jumped in his car, cranked up the sound, and drove off.

Birdie moved toward the door. "Hey! It's fixed already," she said. "Mama can fix anything, Bowser." I'd have to remember that, and maybe I would have if Rory hadn't driven up on his bicycle just then. He tried to pop a wheelie as he turned up our walk, but something wobbly happened and he had to put a foot down real fast.

"Uh, hi, Birdie," he said. "Hey, Bowser."

Rory's a pal, somewhat taller than Birdie. Just like her, he had a strange jumble of teeth, some big, some little. His hair was all over the place, maybe because of bicycle wind. What else about Rory? His father's the sheriff, for one thing. Is that important? I didn't know then, although now I do.

"Hi," Birdie said.

"Hi."

After some silence, Rory said, "How's it goin'?"

"Okay," said Birdie. "You?"

"Not bad."

Then more silence. This was how their conversations usually started, and often ended, too. Rory adjusted one of the rubber grips on his handlebars. Birdie watched him doing it.

"Baseball still going on?" she said.

"Two more games."

"Long season."

"Uh-huh." Rory got busy with the rubber grip on the other side. He took a deep breath. "I'm in a slump."

"You'll come out of it."

Rory looked up quickly. "Yeah? How do you know?"

Birdie shrugged. "That's what a slump means. It's like a hill, a valley, and another hill. You're in the valley."

"What if there's no second hill?"

"Then it's not a slump."

"Meaning I just suck?"

Birdie gazed at Rory. He didn't look happy, but Birdie laughed anyway. And then Rory started laughing, too. They laughed and laughed. Humans can be very difficult to understand.

"Want to come in?" Birdie said. "Have some limeade?"

"Sure," said Rory, getting off his bike. "Heard you got broken into."

"Yeah."

"But nothing got taken."

"That's right. How do you know?"

"My dad was on the police radio. We have it on in the kitchen while he's at work. He's worried about robbers from the city. Sometimes they hit small towns—it happened over in Cleoma last year."

"You know the Richelieus?" Birdie said.

"I know who Preston is."

"Quarterback of the Hornets."

"*Woo-woo*. And one of the best pitchers in the state. Scouts come to watch him."

"So?" Birdie said.

"What's that mean?"

"He's kind of a jerk."

"You've met him?" Rory said.

"Nola and I went over there."

"How come?"

"Because they got broken into and so did we."

Rory nodded. "Yeah. My dad thinks you musta surprised them—the robbers, I mean—which is how come nothing got taken from your place."

Birdie shook her head. "We didn't surprise them—Bowser would have known."

My tail rose up to the sky.

"Uh, my dad didn't mention Bowser," Rory said.

Birdie shrugged.

"But the good thing," Rory went on, "is you didn't lose anything. The Richelieus lost a pearl necklace."

"What?"

"Worth a lot of money, Mrs. Richelieu told my dad. She's real upset."

five

 PEARL NECKLACE?" BIRDIE SAID. HER voice rose, and so did her lovely little eyebrows. "You're sure?"

"Yeah," said Rory. "But don't tell anyone."

"Huh?"

"Because no one's supposed to know."

"You know."

"But I'm not supposed to. It's only 'cause I overheard."

"So?"

"So last time it got my dad in trouble. I overheard then, too, same way."

"Overheard what?"

"That time? It was something about Solange."

"Solange Claymore?"

"Uh-huh. She was getting mixed up with—whoa!" Rory's eyes opened wide, one of those signs of an alarmed human. "I almost did it again!"

"Once you start you have to finish," Birdie said. "Isn't that one of the rules in your family?"

"Rule three," said Rory. He bit his lip. "But I can't, Birdie. Don't make me."

"Then explain better."

"How?"

"Start with the part about getting your dad in trouble."

"With the DA over in Lafayette."

"Is he your dad's boss?"

"It's a she. And my dad has no boss."

"Why not?"

" 'Cause he's elected. So the people are his boss, kinda. But the DA's a big backer of his, and what if she switched to someone else? Like maybe Mr. Santini."

"Mr. Santini who owns the campground?"

"Yeah, but he was a cop in Houston and the DA's from there and knew him back then. And she got real mad the last time—it blew up the whole case."

"A whole case against Solange?"

"She was just a little part of it. What happened was— whoa! Stop making me, Birdie."

"I'm not making you do anything."

"You already did."

"I didn't."

"You did."

Birdie's back stiffened. I could feel my own back doing the same, although my back never really stiffens. Our backs—meaning the backs of me and my kind—are much more relaxed than yours, if you don't mind me saying so.

"That's not true, Rory, and you know it."

He raised a hand. "All right, all right. No need to go to Code Red."

"I didn't."

"You did. And if you mention"—Rory's voice sank real low—"the pearls and my dad finds out—which he will, take it to the bank—then I'll get a whupping."

Birdie backed up a step. "Your dad whups you?"

Rory looked down. "No, not really. Except once or twice."

"Including the Solange thing?"

"Nope. Didn't whup me then 'cause I didn't know it was wrong. But now I do."

"So he'd whup you?"

Rory nodded.

"Like how?"

"What do you mean, like how? You never got whupped?"

Birdie shook her head.

"Guess that's the upside of not having a dad," said Rory.

Silence. A strange silence that seemed to press down from above. And then, in a quiet voice that somehow sounded powerful, like it had picked up that pressure from above, Birdie spoke. "What did you say?"

"I take it back," Rory said, real quick.

"Go away," Birdie said.

"Aw, Birdie, it's just that you got me so—"

"Leave."

Red splotches appeared on Rory's face. He opened his mouth like he was going to say something, closed it, and gave Birdie a mixed-up sort of look, part angry, part hurt, part I didn't know what and maybe he didn't either. Then he pushed off and pedaled away very fast, standing on the pedals instead of sitting on the seat.

We went inside. Mama was at the kitchen table, working on her laptop. She glanced up. "Hi there, Bir—Hey! What's wrong?"

"Nothing," Birdie said, heading toward the hall, me right beside her, which I'm sure you knew already.

"Whoa, right there," Mama said, rising and taking Birdie by the arms in a gentle way. "Your face sure isn't saying *nothing*, sweetheart. It's saying plenty."

Birdie looked away.

"It's the break-in, isn't it?" Mama said. "I understand. I feel the same way. It's a violation. You know what a violation is?"

Birdie nodded.

"Understanding also means moving on," Mama said. "Can't dwell on it, otherwise we'd just be extending the violation. Do you see what I mean?"

56

Birdie nodded again.

"But I sure hope the sheriff catches whatever scummy person did this," Mama said. "And he's optimistic. He sees patterns in the two break-ins, patterns that point to a gang over in Lafayette."

Birdie looked up at Mama. "What patterns?"

"He didn't go into that. But he did say we shouldn't be afraid of a repeat performance. Has that been worrying you?"

Birdie shook her head.

"Because that's not how these gangs operate. They hit random places, grab what they can, and take off down the road, never to return." Mama gazed down at Birdie. "Any questions?"

"No."

"I think I still see a question or two," Mama said.

"Impossible," Birdie said.

"Oh?"

"I've got a poker face."

Mama laughed. "Not to me you don't." She wrapped her arms around Birdie and squeezed her tight. "Not to me you don't." Mama's eyes closed. Birdie's, still open, looked worried. I moved in to break up the hug, my only thought at that moment, but when you have a time-tested thought like that in your repertoire you don't need any more.

"How about looking in on Grammy?" Mama said, after I'd gotten our positioning all sorted out. "She's having a little rest."

"In the middle of the day?" Birdie said.

"Well, she's supposed to be having a little rest," Mama said. "Orders of Dr. Rajatawan. But he . . . he doesn't have quite the right way with her."

"How come he wants her to rest?" Birdie said. "I thought he was just worried about the pills."

"That too," Mama said.

"What's wrong with Grammy? Tell me!"

"I don't want you to worry."

"That only makes me worry more."

Mama laughed. Then her face got all serious and she said, "Grammy's heart's not getting the job done quite how Dr. Rajatawan would like."

"But won't the pills fix that?" Birdie said. "If she'll only take them in the right way?"

Mama gazed down at Birdie. From the look in Mama's eyes, I thought tears were on the way, but that didn't happen. "That would help, for sure," she said, her voice a little thick, like something had clogged her throat.

We crossed the breezeway, me and Birdie, entered Grammy's side of the house, and came to her bedroom

58

door. I could hear Grammy moving around on the other side, moving kind of briskly. I'd always thought rest meant not moving briskly, but I might have gotten that wrong. Birdie knocked.

"Come in, for pity's sake, child," Grammy called.

Birdie opened the door. "How'd you know it was me, Grammy?"

"Think I don't know your knock?" Grammy said. She glanced over from what she was doing, which involved a broom and a small grate in the ceiling above her bed. Grammy stood beside the bed, up on her tiptoes, sort of shoving the end of the broom handle into the square spaces in the grate, and grunting with the effort. Cool air flowed out of the grate. Was Grammy trying to make it flow faster? That was my only idea, but a pretty good one, as I hope you agree.

"Grammy?"

"What now?"

"Um, what are you doing?" Birdie said.

"Exactly what it"—grunt—"looks like."

"Sticking the broom handle in that thingy?"

"Vent is the"—grunt—"word. That 'thingy,' as you put it, is an AC vent. Learn the names of what's around—don't they teach you that in school?"

"I don't think so," Birdie said.

"Should have known," said Grammy.

"Is something wrong with the vent?"

"Would I be going to all this effort if it wasn't?"

"No, Grammy. But aren't you supposed to be resting?"

Grammy stopped what she was doing, came down off her tiptoes—she was barefoot, maybe a fact I should have mentioned before, especially since her toes seemed all swollen and bruised—and turned to Birdie. "Not you too. Don't even start. And as for you," she said, suddenly looking my way, "sit!"

I sat. Sort of. There's an almost-sit I can do that allows for a tiny bit of movement at the same time. It seemed to be good enough. Birdie glanced at Grammy's desk, crowded with pill bottles.

"What games do you like, Grammy?" she said.

"Games? Games? What kind of nonsense question is that?"

"You must like some sort of game," said Birdie.

"Where does it say that?"

"Nowhere, I guess. But . . . but you like fishing, for example."

"You think fishing's a game?"

Birdie looked down. "No."

"Darn straight. Nothin' more serious than fishing. This family has depended on fishing since . . . since I don't even know when. That's how long!" Grammy got back to work, poking the broom handle in the vent.

"What's wrong with the vent?" Birdie said.

"You don't hear that infernal racket?"

"Racket?"

"Coming from the grate."

Birdie cocked an ear up toward the grate, shook her head.

"Like something's fluttering around in there?" Grammy said.

I heard that fluttering, loud and clear. Meaning Grammy and I were hearing something and Birdie wasn't? That bothered me, and was still bothering me when I heard a click from somewhere below the floor and the cool air stopped flowing, the fluttering sound stopping as well.

"You really don't hear it?" Grammy said. "Been like this since that thunderstorm last week."

"Thunderstorm?"

"Don't tell me you slept through it."

"I must have."

"That last boom shook the house like the roof was fixin' to fly right off." She gave Birdie a look. "Wasted on the young."

"What is, Grammy?"

"Nothing." Grammy cocked her ear up to the vent,

silent now. A puzzled look appeared on her face. "Hrrmf," she said and leaned the broom against the wall.

Birdie eyed the pills. "Speaking of games, Grammy, what do you think about basketball?"

Grammy got a faraway look in her washed-out eyes. "I was deadly," she said in a soft voice.

Birdie's face lit up. "From the three-point line, Grammy?"

"Three-point line? There was no three-point line when I played."

"No three-point line?"

"Just another one of those stupid improvements that make things worse."

Birdie was silent. I could feel her thoughts, so pleasant, especially since I didn't seem to be having any of my own just then. "I think you're right," she said, "at least about the three-point shot."

"Of course I'm right. Takes the *team* right out of *teamwork*."

"I never thought about that," Birdie said.

"And now you don't have to—all the thinking's done." Grammy glanced up at the vent and frowned.

Birdie cleared her throat. That's sort of an announcement from humans that something important is on the way. "Funny how we can make up games, huh, Grammy?"

"What on earth are you talking about?"

"Well, for example, we could kind of play basketball in miniature, if we got creative."

Grammy's eyes narrowed. "Spit it out, whatever little plot you've got going on."

Birdie's eyes shifted for a second or two. Then she laughed. "Stop, Grammy."

"Stop what? Being me?"

"Oh, no," Birdie said. "It's just that I've thought of a game we could play. You could play, really, is what I mean. And I'll keep score."

Grammy folded her arms across her chest. "Go on."

Birdie cleared her throat again. "You know the way Snoozy tosses jujubes way up in the air and catches them in his mouth?"

"Just another one of his disgusting habits."

Birdie spoke faster. "I thought we could play the same sort of game, only . . ."

"Only what?"

Birdie turned to the desk. "Only with those pills. You doing the . . . the shooting, and me counting the baskets. Our own little game, Grammy."

Grammy's face got kind of complicated. Around the mouth she looked angry, but her eyes seemed about to cry. Had I ever seen Grammy cry? Not that I remembered, and wouldn't I remember something like that? In the end, she didn't cry, and when she spoke she didn't sound real angry, at least not for her.

"That's the dumbest idea I've ever heard," she said. "But I'll take the stupid pills at the right stupid time." She shook her finger at Birdie. "And in the normal way. Meaning with a glass of water. I wasn't brought up in a barn, unlike some others I could name. Now scoot."

We scooted. When we were out on the breezeway, Grammy's door safely closed behind us, I could still hear her. "Snoozy! Jujubes!"

OW DID THAT GO?" MAMA SAID,
glancing up from her laptop.

"Pretty good, I think," said Birdie. Mama
looked surprised. Then Birdie said, "What's the wellhead
price?" And Mama looked even more surprised.

"You mean right now, this very moment?"

"Um, yeah, sure."

Mama tapped at the screen. "Surprised you even know
the term." She frowned. "Good grief—down another two
and a quarter. Why is it cratering like this?"

"Mama? Is something wrong? What's cratering?"

"There's no way Houston's going to just sit there and
take these losses. I can't believe how fast—"

Mama's phone beeped. She checked its little screen and
right away lost most of the color from her face.

"Mama?"

Mama slowly rose and gathered up her shoulder bag,
which was hanging over a chair. "I—I'll be back in a bit,"
she said.

"Where are you going?" Birdie said.

"The Lafayette office," Mama said. "Two-thirty meeting."

"But I thought you were off for three weeks," said Birdie.

"An unanticipated meeting." Mama dropped her phone in her bag and headed for the door.

"Unanticipated?"

"Not on the schedule."

"So . . . um?"

"We'll just have to see." Mama shot Birdie a quick smile—quick and real small. Then she was out the door. Clunk of the car door, *vroom-vroom* of the motor starting up, and then she peeled away, coming real close to burning rubber. That's a special sound that happens when the rubber's heating up but not yet burning, a faint screech my ears can pick up, don't know about yours.

Birdie moved over to the table, peered at Mama's computer. "Just a whole bunch of graphs," she said. "All these graphs and numbers. They must mean something but . . ." She sat down, tapped at the keyboard. "Wellhead price . . . hmm. Says here it's the price of oil or natural gas right when it comes out of the ground and before any transportation or . . . Kind of complicated, Bowser." Birdie gave me a pat. I was under the table by that time, sitting on her feet, which was my go-to position for surfing the Internet. "So if the price is cheaper won't more people use it? Then they'll sell more and Houston will be happy? But Mama didn't look happy." She closed the computer. No more surfing? A real short session, in my experience. "And all this on top of the break-in."

Birdie went to the fridge, took out the jug of limeade, poured herself a glass. Birdie loves limeade, especially the limeade Grammy makes from the limes that grow on our own lime tree, out back. Once, on a day Grammy and I were really getting along—this was earlier in the summer, back when everyone was still calling ol' Bowser a hero for saving Birdie from terrible danger in the swamp, the details now foggy in my mind—she, meaning Grammy, started to teach me how to bring her any limes that had fallen to the ground. She even put one in her own mouth! And said, "See, like this, for mercy's sake!" As if I didn't know how to snap up a lime! The truth was I was playing a little game of my own with Grammy. But then, just as we were getting along so well, me and Grammy with limes in our mouths and maybe at the beginning of a whole new relationship, who should happen by but a squirrel? A squirrel sauntering across our private property and me in charge of security, if you see where I'm going with this. What happened after that is blurry, somehow ending in a taxi ride from Minville, the next town down the bayou. The first and only—so far!—taxi ride of my career, me all by myself in the backseat and the driver glancing nervously in the rearview mirror, for reasons unknown to me. Did the ride turn out to be a bit pricey? I'm pretty sure Grammy said some things to the driver that I'd never heard before. Our whole new relationship didn't get off the ground, so even to this day we're pretty much right where we used to be.

But back to the limeade. The smell of Birdie's limeade, some now dripping off her chin—how thirsty she got sometimes!—reminded me of lime aftershave, and how the house had smelled so strongly of it after the break-in. And not only lime aftershave, but of cat as well. Cat? Why would—

"Oh, Bowser," Birdie said, setting down her glass. "I'm worried."

What was this? Birdie worried? I forgot about everything else.

"It's like we're . . . we're caught in a trap," she went on.

Caught in a trap? Like one of the crab traps Grammy keeps in her own special place on the lake? I'd never heard of anything so horrible. Me and Birdie wriggling around with all those blue crabs? I'd never even had a nightmare that bad. Uh-oh. Now maybe I would.

"Don't pant, Bowser," Birdie said. "If you're thirsty, go drink."

Thirsty? I wasn't the least bit thirsty, but since I always cut Birdie some slack, I went over to my bowl in the corner

68

and took a sip. And then another and another until I was licking the bowl dry. Right away, I felt so much better, in fact, just about perfect. Birdie knew me better than I knew me! So with her around I didn't need to even bother knowing me, could reserve all my mental energy for other things. What a break!

"How about a walk?" Birdie said. "We need to think."

I needed to think? Wow. Hadn't realized that. But there's nothing like a walk. I was already at the door.

"Don't scratch on the door, Bowser!"

If that was happening, I put a stop to it at once. Scratching on the door is a violation of security, and you know who's in charge of security around these parts.

"It's the pearls, Bowser," Birdie said as we went by the high school. School hadn't started yet, but I'd heard something about how I myself wouldn't be going. Just Birdie. I hoped I'd heard wrong. Meanwhile, even though school hadn't started, the football team was out there practicing, some of them in yellow jerseys, the rest in black. All except for two or three, who wore red.

"Red for the quarterbacks," Birdie said. "No hitting the quarterbacks in practice." Birdie knew everything! What was a quarterback? I had no idea. As we went by, one of the quarterbacks, his face mostly hidden by his helmet and faceguard, seemed to see us.

"Speak of the devil," Birdie said. "That'll be Preston Richelieu."

Preston turned our way, made his hand like a gun, and pulled the trigger. Hey! I remembered that from before. Hadn't liked it the first time.

"What a jerk!" Birdie said, not loudly. "Think he knows anything?"

Nothing. Preston knew diddly-squat, as far as I was concerned. We turned a corner, headed down a dirt road, a little patch of blue bayou shining at the end.

"The sheriff thinks the pearls got taken, Bowser, but they didn't get taken," Birdie said. "Which we know, thanks to you."

Wow! Really? Tell me more.

"So he needs to know, because . . . because all sorts of things. Like why would the Richelieus report a theft if there was no theft? And what's the connection with the break-in at our place? It's important, Bowser. But what are we going to do?"

Take a quick dip in the bayou? That was the only solution that came to me at the moment.

"It's only 'cause of Rory that we know the pearls are supposed to be missing," Birdie was saying. "If we just up and tell Sheriff Cannon, Rory'll get whupped, and the DA in Lafayette'll stop supporting the sheriff, and we'll end up with Mr. Santini from the campground as the sheriff. That would be bad. I happen to know he hates kids, won't allow family campers on his property." She gave me a sideways look. "Not fond of dogs, either."

Not fond of dogs? I tried to figure out what that meant, couldn't quite get there.

"So we need a way for the sheriff to . . . to find out on his own! That's it, Bowser!" She turned and gave me a very vigorous pat. "You're a genius! That's the solution. Now we just fill in the blanks."

What was this? I was a genius? Sounded good. I hoped to find out what it meant one day. By this time we were walking on the path by the bayou. Up ahead rose the Lucinda Street Bridge. The food truck was gone but a kid was fishing from the top of the bridge, a skinny kid with a dark tan and a Mohawk haircut.

"Hey, Junior," Birdie said as we walked onto the bridge.

"Hey," said Junior Tebbets, jiggling his bamboo pole.

"You fish without a reel?" Birdie said.

"Why not?"

"Catching anything?"

"Nope."

"What're you fishing for?"

"Catfish."

"What bait?"

Junior peered over the railing. His line hung straight down, disappeared into the water. "Mouse."

"I'm sorry?"

"Dead mouse," Junior said.

"You're using a dead mouse for bait?"

"Like, wouldn't it be kind of cruel to hook 'em live?" Junior said. "Found this one under the truck when my dad drove away."

"Under the food truck?" Birdie said.

"Scooped it right up. Everyone knows catfish go for stinky things."

"Then everyone knows wrong," Birdie said. "Shiners is what they like."

"Shiners?" Junior jiggled the pole. That made tiny waves down in the bayou, but no fish appeared.

"Hang on," Birdie said. We hurried down off the bridge. Why? I had no clue, but when Birdie hurries I hurry. In moments we were on the dock that starts up along the bayou just beyond the bridge and not long after that we came to Gaux Family Fish and Bait. We woke up Snoozy, asleep on the porch couch, Birdie giving him a little push toward the door, and then Birdie grabbed a small pail full of tiny silvery fishes, and we were back to the bridge in no time. Who was more fun than Birdie?

Junior turned to us. "Thought maybe I had a bite there for a sec—"

Birdie took his bamboo pole and with one little flick of her wrist whipped the line up out of the water in an easy slow-motion sort of way. Something not-too-pleasant-looking dangled from a hook at the end of the line, but it fell off in midair and plopped into the bayou.

"There goes my bait!" Junior said.

"Small mercies," said Birdie.

"Small mercies? What does that mean?"

Birdie shrugged. "Something my grammy says." Birdie reached into the pail and grabbed—gently but firmly—a little silvery fish, wriggling and squirmy. She held it out for Junior. "Here," she said.

"Here what?" said Junior.

"Hook 'im up," Birdie told him.

"How?"

"You don't know how to hook up a shiner? What you want is to slip the hook in under the lower jaw like so, and make the point come through about"—grunt—"here. Haven't really hurt the shiner, meaning he'll be more lively."

"What makes you so sure you haven't hurt him?" Junior said. "Looks kind of painful to me."

Birdie flicked the bamboo pole, and the shiner, now hooked to the end of the line, arced down into the bayou, making a small splash and then swimming underwater and out of sight.

"I thought you were tough," Birdie said.

"Me?" said Junior. "I'm an artist. Can you read music, by the way?"

"No."

"Because it'll be good if someone in the band reads music."

"Who's in the band?"

"So far? You and me. There's plenty that wants to join, of course, but I'm picky when it comes to—"

"Shh."

"Huh?"

"Don't scare the fish," Birdie said, her voice low.

"What fish?" said Junior, gazing down. No fish to see, just the line hanging motionless, the water smooth and undisturbed.

Birdie wasn't gazing down. In fact, her eyes were half-closed, her head turned slightly, like she was listening for something. "That's it, Mr. Catfish," she said, sort of like she was talking to herself. "Just settle down for a nice big chomp."

"You're acting weird," Junior said.

Uh-oh. Had Junior just said something mean about Birdie? If so, it was my job to—

"Yeah," said Birdie, her eyes opening, her voice starting to rise. "Just . . . like . . . that!" And then, with a tremendous heave, both hands on the pole, Birdie heaved, and from up out of the bayou rose an enormous fish, thrashing back and forth at the end of the line. "Grab on!"

"Me?"

"I'm going to throw you in, Junior."

Moving real quick, Junior grabbed on to the pole, skinny muscles straining in his skinny arms.

"Pull!" Birdie said.

Junior pulled. Birdie pulled. I ran around in small circles, very fast. The fish topped the bridge railing, got swung around, came slowly down to the pavement.

"Wow!" Junior said. "What's it weigh?"

"Don't know," Birdie said. "Let's take it to the shop and—"

She paused. A big red cruiser with black trim was passing under the bridge from up the bayou, the engine doing a slow and powerful *THROOM-THROOM-THROOM*. First the bow appeared—you work at Gaux Family Fish and Bait for any time at all, as I have, and you learn boating lingo— then the cabin, followed by a console with a man at the controls, face hidden by the brim of a big straw hat, and finally a deck at the stern. A woman sat on the deck, a drink in her hand, her purse beside her. She seemed to be watching the man, possibly in an annoyed way, to judge by her eyes, both of them gooped up with so much makeup I could smell it. Hey! It was Miranda Richelieu. And now

I could see the man's face, a heavy sort of face with thick eyebrows: her husband, Merv.

Miranda opened her purse, took out a pack of cigarettes, lit one up.

"Junior," Birdie whispered. "Have you got a camera?"

"A camera?"

"Shh! A phone. Quick, Junior! Anything to take a picture."

"Nope," said Junior, also whispering. "Picture of what?"

"The purse."

"What about it?"

"Look inside!"

"I see a gold lighter."

"Under it!"

Junior squinted. "Maybe a . . . necklace?"

"Made of?"

By now the cruiser was some distance away. Junior squinted harder. "Hard to say."

"Pearls?" Birdie said.

Junior shrugged. "Maybe pearls. What's the big deal? My mom has a pearl necklace. And my stepmom."

The red cruiser sped up, rounded a bend, and disappeared from view, its spreading wake petering out on the banks of the bayou.

"And my stepmom before her," Junior said.

seven

JUNIOR WENT TO PICK UP THE CATFISH, BUT
it slipped from his hands and flopped back down.

"Between the gills, Junior," Birdie said. "Get
hold between the gills."

"These things here?"

"Yeah. You act like you've never fished before."

"I've fished plenty," Junior said. "I just don't know all
the names."

"Learn the names of what's around," Birdie said, but so
softly I barely heard it myself.

"Huh?" said Junior.

"Nothing," Birdie said. She scooped up the catfish.
Junior slung the bamboo pole over his bony shoulder. We
started off the bridge, the catfish still wriggling a bit, but
its smell starting to change from living to something that
was not, a change I pick up on right away. Meanwhile, the
Lucinda Street light switched to green and a motorcycle
came through the intersection and drove onto the bridge.
The motorcycle, dusty and dented, with a dusty and dented
guitar case strapped on the back, slowed as it passed us.

The driver turned to look our way. "You kids see a boat go by?" she called out over the engine noise.

"Huh?" Junior said. Birdie put a hand to her ear. Meaning what? She and Junior hadn't heard the question? I'd caught it, loud and clear.

The driver cut the engine, slipped off the bike with a nice easy motion, stood it on the kickstand, and came our way. She took off her helmet and shook out her hair. Hey! This was Snoozy's customer from yesterday, the woman who'd shown lots of interest in his arm tattoos but hadn't ended up spending one red cent, if I remembered right. Now I got a good close-up look at her. She was quite a bit younger than Mama and quite a bit older than Birdie, which was as far as I could go on the matter of age. And, yes, I loved that hair: short and dark on one side, long and bright green on the other. Her eyes were green, too, and also bright, like she was excited about something. Those green eyes went to Birdie, made a quick examination of Junior, and settled back on Birdie.

"Hi," said the young woman. "What you got there?"

"Catfish," said Birdie.

"It's so big!"

"We both caught it," Junior said.

"Cool," said the young woman. "You caught it from up here on the bridge?"

"Yup," said Junior. "Using shiners for bait. That's how we roll with catfish, right, Birdie?"

"Did you happen—" The young woman began, and then paused, her green eyes shifted slightly, like they were getting tugged by some thought inside. "Your name's Birdie?"

Birdie nodded.

"Great name," the young woman said. "I'm Drea Bolden."

"I'm Junior," Junior said. "Junior Tebbets."

"Nice to meet you," said Drea Bolden. She gave Birdie a smile, maybe bigger than the normal friendly size. "And what's your last name, Birdie?"

"Gaux," Birdie said.

"Ah," said Drea. Then she turned to me. "Who's this handsome dude?"

Finally! What a long time she'd taken before getting to me! But in the end, she'd come up big. I decided I liked Drea.

"Bowser," Birdie said.

"Think he'll let me pat him?"

"I'd bet anything," said Birdie.

Drea laughed and gave me a pat. Always nice to be on the receiving end of a pat, although Drea's pat didn't do much for me. Some humans don't have a lot of patting experience, patting you the way they'd pat a pillow, just doing a job. Drea's pat was like that. But no complaints.

Drea glanced over the rail. "Did you kids happen to see a boat go by?"

"What kind of boat?" Birdie said.

"I'm not good with boat types," Drea said.

"There was a thirty-two-foot cabin cruiser, maybe a little longer, a few minutes ago," Birdie said. "Red with black trim. It said *Cardinal* on the stern."

"But you, on the other hand," Drea said, "know a thing or two about boats."

"She should," said Junior. "The Gaux own Gaux Family Fish and Bait."

"Ah," said Drea. She put her helmet on, turned toward the motorcycle.

"That a guitar in the case?" Junior said.

"It is."

"You play?"

"Some."

"Know how to read music?"

"I do."

"And write down a tune if you hear it?"

Drea nodded. "What's up, Junior?"

"I get these tunes in my head, but then forget them," Junior said. "We're putting a band together, me and Birdie."

"Well," Birdie said. "I'm not—"

"What do you play, Junior?"

"Drums."

"My first guess," Drea said.

"And Birdie sings," Junior said.

"Well, I don't really . . ."

Drea's bright green eyes brightened a little more. "Tell you what," she said. "I could write down one or two of your tunes if you drop by a little later, say around four."

"Drop by where?" said Junior.

"I'm staying at the campground. Green tent by the pond."

"Santini's Campground?" Birdie said.

"You come, too," Drea said, getting on the bike. "I'll sing the harmony to your melody." She cranked the motor, wheeled around, and rode over the bridge, turning onto the road that ran next to the bayou path and zooming off in the same direction the red cruiser had gone. *Cardinal?* Was that the name? So much to keep track of!

"What's harmony?" Junior said. "Or . . . what's the other one? Melody?"

Birdie shrugged. The catfish kind of shrugged, too, giving one more little tail flutter and then hanging limp from Birdie's hand.

"Can I keep it?" Junior said.

"The fish?"

"Get in good with my dad. He'll make a blackened po'boy out of it."

"Get in good with your dad?" Birdie said.

Junior nodded, not meeting her gaze.

"Sure," Birdie said. "It's all yours."

We took the catfish over to the shop. Birdie woke Snoozy. He weighed the catfish. "Fifteen pounds, six ounces. Not too shabby." Snoozy packed the catfish on ice, gave it to Junior. Junior went home, and so did we.

Grammy was out sweeping the breezeway floor, sweeping it in a severe sort of way, as though it had gotten her mad.

"Looks like you're feeling better, Grammy," Birdie said.

"Wasn't feeling poorly in the first place."

"Um, good," Birdie said. "Good news."

"Not news where I come from," Grammy said. "News should be new. Nothing new about feeling how you always feel."

"Grammy?"

"Out with it."

"What do we know about the Richelieus?"

"Never spoken to them in my life."

"They were the other people who got broken into."

"So I hear," Grammy said.

"They just went out on their boat."

"Thirty-five-foot cabin cruiser, twin Merc three-fifty diesels?"

"I thought you didn't know them," Birdie said.

"Lots of people I don't know in this neck of the woods," said Grammy. "But I know all the boats."

"What does a boat like theirs cost?"

"Depends. New? Used? Condition? Rigged how?" Grammy shook her finger. "But always remember one thing."

"I know, Grammy. A boat is a hole in the ocean into which you throw money."

Grammy nodded. "Don't you forget."

"I won't, Grammy," Birdie said. "What do the Richelieus do?"

"Do?"

"To make money."

"Couldn't tell you," Grammy said. "They live here but they're not from here. Biloxi, maybe? Or is she from Cleoma originally?"

"That's only five miles away."

"Five long miles," Grammy said. "And I believe he's from New Orleans."

"Their son, Preston, is quarterback of the Hornets."

"So what?"

"Not 'so what,' Grammy. Whenever anyone says Hornets you're supposed to say *woo-woo*."

"That was stupid back then and it's still stupid."

"What do you mean 'back then'?" Birdie said.

Grammy got busy with the broom, did some more angry sweeping. I'm a big fan of sweeping. For one thing, it can stir up smells you didn't even know were there. In this case, I learned something brand-new and maybe a little disturbing: We had a snake under our breezeway. And not a small one, if you could judge by the size of the scent. I'm not a fan of snakes, and from one or two past encounters, I knew that they're not fans of me.

"Think I don't know about the Hornets?" Grammy said. "Sat in the stands for every game, four years running, back in the day."

"You were a football fan, Grammy?"

"Pah! Hated the game then and hate it now. But your daddy was the quarterback."

"He was?"

"Calm under pressure," Grammy said. "That's what made him good."

"I . . . I never knew that. About him playing in high school. In fact, there's so much I . . . I don't know about him. How come?"

"How come what?" Grammy said. "And what do you think you're doing, buster?"

Buster? I knew no Busters. What I knew was that we had us a snake under the breezeway floor at 19 Gentilly

Lane, where I just happened to be in charge of security. That meant I had to start digging a hole under the narrow strip of trellis that covered the space between the ground and the breezeway floor—a nice, substantial hole that would bring me face-to-face with the culprit so I could let him know what's what. Any job worth doing is worth doing well, as I'd heard Grammy herself say more than once, meaning if big chunks of lawn were flying around, it was all for the best, nothing to see here, folks, just a working dude at his—

"WHOA!" Grammy yelled. How amazingly loud she could be for someone so old and small! I looked at her in surprise, and found that she seemed to be looking at me, and in a fierce sort of way, like . . . like something was wrong. I couldn't think what, so I got right back to work, using all my paws to make up for the lost time. What fun to have all four paws in action at—

"Bowser?" Birdie said quietly, her hand on my collar, not hard. "How about a little time-out?"

Time-out? That meant going inside the house and having a treat. Treat yes, in the house no. That was my position.

Not long after that—maybe pretty soon after—I found myself in the kitchen. We were sitting around the table,

Grammy, Birdie, and me. They sat in chairs. I sat at Birdie's feet, waiting for my treat.

"What has he done to deserve a treat?" Grammy said.

"He did come inside," said Birdie.

"Dragged at the end of a leash."

I wondered briefly who they were talking about, then squeezed closer to Birdie, just in case I'd slipped her mind. Grammy gave me a glance that might not have been her friendliest, then sipped her ice tea.

"As for your father," she said, "the fact is, you're only eleven. When you were ready, you'd ask. That was how I saw it, and your mama, too."

"I'm ready," Birdie said.

"Ask away."

Birdie closed her eyes for a moment. I loved when she did that! It meant she was thinking her deepest thoughts. A good time for me to think my deepest thoughts along with her, which I did: *Treats!*

Birdie's eyes opened. So blue today, like she had the sky inside her. She turned to Grammy. "Am I like him?" she said.

Grammy grunted, maybe in surprise, and shook her head.

"I'm not?" Birdie said. "Not at all?"

Grammy shook her head again. "Quite the reverse," she said. "That there—'am I like him?'—is just the kind of question he'd ask. Question number one always came first with him."

"I don't understand," Birdie said.

"Point being it's uncanny sometimes," Grammy said. She sipped more tea, seemed to be having deep thoughts of her own.

"Um," Birdie said, "I know he was small like me when he was a kid."

"Who told you that?" Grammy said.

"Snoozy's uncle Lem."

"Lem LaChance? One-man revenue stream for every bar in town?"

"I don't know about that, Grammy. But he told me he coached peewee football back then—"

"A disgrace right there."

"—and my daddy was one of the smallest players."

"At least he's got one clear memory," Grammy said. "Robert—that was your father's name, Robert Lee Gaux—"

"I know that, Grammy."

"Don't interrupt," Grammy said. "Robert didn't come into his size until the summer before senior year at the high school."

"Will it be the same for me?" Birdie said.

"Do I look like a seer?" Grammy said.

"What's a seer?"

"Someone who can see the future."

Birdie cocked her head, maybe checking out Grammy from a different angle. I do the same thing myself. "I think so, Grammy."

"Ain't no seers in this life, child, and don't you forget it."

"I won't."

Grammy glanced at her watch. "More questions? Snoozy's shift is over in twenty minutes. And he better be wide awake when I get there."

"Well," Birdie said, "what about the medal?"

Grammy gazed into her glass, poked at the lemon slice floating in the tea. "No comfort there," she said. "It's just a thing."

Birdie nodded. "But how did he win it?"

"Win? Win? He won the medal, if that's how you want to put it, by getting killed in the line of duty. Chief presented it to your mama at the funeral." Grammy rose, patted her hair in the mirror, and headed to the door.

"But what happened, Grammy?" Birdie said.

"I don't understand you," Grammy said, her hand on the doorknob.

"What happened in the line of duty?"

Grammy turned. "He was working on a murder case. I don't remember all the details, if I ever knew them in the first place."

"In New Orleans?"

" 'Course, New Orleans. That's where he and your mama lived in the beginning, and you too. It was only after that you came up here."

"Did the case end up getting solved?"

"What case?"

"That last case. The one he was working on."

"Most certainly not," Grammy said. "Some might say what difference does it make. But I'm here to tell you—"

All at once the door opened from the outside, bumping Grammy's arm, and in came Mama.

"Oh, sorry," Mama said. Her gaze went to Birdie, over at the table, and back to Grammy. Mama's face looked pale, and her eyes seemed very big and very dark.

"Mama?" Birdie said. "Is something wrong?"

Mama smiled, a stiff kind of smile, like she was making it happen. "Not really," she said. "Not in the long term."

"But in the short term?" Grammy said.

"In the short term," Mama said, "they closed down the whole division, effective today. Can't make money at these prices, not on the deep-sea rigs. The numbers are the numbers."

Birdie rose. I rose, too, stood beside her. "What does 'close down the whole division' mean?"

Mama's smile, what there was of it, vanished completely.

She almost looked as though she was angry at Birdie, which made no sense. But humans didn't always make sense, not in my experience. "They fired one hundred and fifty-three people," Mama said.

"Including you, Mama?"

"Number forty-seven on the list," Mama said. "It was in alphabetical order."

eight

ILENCE FELL IN OUR LITTLE KITCHEN. SO
many different silences in life! This kind was all
about waiting to see what happens next.

"How about a glass of tea?" Grammy said.

"Thank you," said Mama, going to the table and sitting down, somewhat heavily, as though her legs had
gotten weak.

"A glass for your mama, please," Grammy told Birdie,
who went to the cupboard and brought back a glass. So
tea was the answer? Tea was happening next? I've tried tea
cold and I've tried tea hot—both times on private excur-
sions in the kitchen—and it did nothing for me. Water is
the drink for me and my kind.

They sat at the table. Mama spooned sugar in her tea.
She still looked pale, and now so did Birdie. Grammy's
face, pale most of the time, seemed to have plenty of color
all of a sudden. She raised her glass, clinked it against
Mama's.

"Here's to the oil business," she said.

Birdie's eyebrows—the tidiest little eyebrows you'd ever

want to see—rose straight up, but Mama laughed and gave Grammy's glass a clink in return.

"We've handled much worse than this," Grammy said.

"True enough," said Mama.

"And come through smelling like roses."

Wow! Something to look forward to! Were all of them going to smell like roses, or just Grammy? Right now, Grammy smelled mostly like dried-up old newspapers, Mama smelled like this special yellow soap she used to get the oil out from under her fingernails, and Birdie smelled of the partially chewed strawberry gum she was storing behind her ear for the moment. All of them smelled slightly of fresh sweat, as well, what with the heat and humidity we've got at this time of year. As for roses, not a trace.

"So," Birdie said, "we'll be all right?"

Mama and Grammy turned to her. "Count on it," Mama said.

"But what about money?"

"Nothing for you to worry about," Mama said. "I've already started putting my résumé out there and I've got a ton of contacts in the industry."

"Okay," said Birdie. Mama reached across the table and patted Birdie's hand. "Except," Birdie went on, "if the wellhead price stays low, who's going to be hiring?"

"Ha!" said Grammy.

Mama gave Grammy an annoyed look. "What does that mean?"

"Nothing," Grammy said. "The kid asked a shrewd question, that's all."

"So?" said Mama. "Is there any point in worrying her?"

"No," said Grammy. "My mistake." She tapped her glass with her fingernail. "Birdie?"

"Yes, Grammy?"

"Don't you worry now, hear? Even if it takes your Mama a bit of time to find something new, we can rely on the business indefinitely."

"The business?" Birdie said.

"Gaux Family Fish and Bait, of course—what we've always relied on, hell or high water. And of high water we've had plenty."

"What does 'indefinitely' mean?" Birdie said.

"Like for the foreseeable future," said Grammy. "And has anyone ever told you that you ask too many darn questions?"

"You have," Birdie said. "Um, Grammy?"

"Um what?" said Grammy.

"The business."

"What about it?"

"Well," Birdie said, "we haven't had a swamp tour since last Tuesday. And also, no one's buying any bait."

"Ha!" said Mama.

Grammy turned to Mama with an annoyed look of her own, a much sharper one than Mama's, since Grammy's face was so sharp to begin with. "What does that mean?"

"Nothing," Mama said. "Just another dose of shrewdness."

"Very funny," said Grammy. But then she laughed, a small laugh that grew a lot bigger. Mama started laughing, too. Birdie looked kind of amazed at first, but she ended up joining in. The three of them laughed and laughed. What were they laughing about? If I'd been following right, we were in a bad way of some sort. So therefore I mustn't have been following right, because humans don't get all laughy when they're in a bad way. Meaning we were in a good way, situation normal. I found myself in the best of all possible moods.

"Bowser!" Mama said. "Paws off the table this second!"

"I've heard stories about the campground," Birdie said.

"Uh-huh," said Junior. "Got any gum?"

"Just this." Birdie took out the wad from behind her ear.

"I'll take it."

"You can have half."

Junior took half. Birdie put the rest back behind her ear. Junior blew a big bubble, filling the air with the smell of strawberry. "What kind of stories?"

We turned down a dirt road, fields full of tall greenish cane stalks on both sides. The strawberry smell got overwhelmed by the smell of sugar.

"About Mr. Santini," Birdie said. "He doesn't sound friendly."

"Got a song about that," Junior said.

"You've got a song about Mr. Santini?"

"Nope. Don't even know him. The song's called 'Stay Away, Friend.' Another Junior Tebbets original, words and lyrics."

"Words are lyrics," Birdie said.

"Yeah? That's how come I need you in the band, right there." Junior reached up into a green stalk that grew by the roadside and tore off a piece from the top. He broke it in two and handed half to Birdie.

"That's stealing," she said.

"From who?" said Junior.

"Whoever owns this cane field."

"Who's that?"

"I don't know. Maybe some neighbor."

"Or some big company from China," Junior said.

"China? Who told you that?"

Junior sucked at the end of his sugarcane for a moment or two, then held it like a microphone. After that came some singing. Junior didn't have a particularly loud voice but it was amazingly harsh to my ears. "Don't you knock, this is the end, you're a loser, stay away, friend." He took a sidelong glance at Birdie. "What do you think?"

"I hate it," Birdie said.

"Oh," said Junior.

"But it's kind of good in a way."

"Yeah? What way?"

"Not mine," Birdie said.

"But could you sing it?" Junior said.

"No."

We came to a gate. It was open, so we went through. To one side stood an entrance booth with no one in the window, and beyond were several gravel lanes leading through the trees, RVs parked here and there. A sign was nailed to a tree at the beginning of each lane. Birdie read them: "Heavenly Road. Paradise Way. Glory Street."

"She just told us a green tent by the pond," Junior said.

"I don't see a pond."

Neither did I, although there was no missing its smell. And wasn't it obvious that the middle lane would take us right there?

"How about Glory Street?" Junior said.

"Why not?" said Birdie.

And they turned toward one of the side lanes. I stood where I was, even digging in a little, and barked.

"Come on, Bowser."

Nope. I barked again. And maybe I'd have started up on a nice long round of barking—so refreshing to get that out of your system every once in a while—except at that moment a man stepped out from behind the entrance booth, a pitchfork in his hand. He was a little potbellied sort of dude but the pitchfork was big, with sharp, gleaming points.

"What in heck is going on here?" he said, his voice rising.

"Maybe you can help us," said Junior.

"Help you?" said the man. "You're kids. And this is a dog."

"Bowser!" Birdie said. "Shh."

Shh? I had some trouble remembering what that meant. Hard to do my best thinking with that pitchfork so near.

The man's voice, kind of high to begin with, rose some more. "No kids here. No dogs. Period."

"Uh, Mr. Santini?" Birdie said. "We just—"

"How do you know my name?"

"You came into our store once," Birdie said. And then to me, "Bowser!"

Uh-oh. Did Birdie sound the tiniest bit angry? Angry at me? That was unbearable. I got a grip on myself, the hardest grip to get, in my experience, and went silent.

"Store?" Mr. Santini was saying. "What store?"

"Gaux Family Fish and Bait," Birdie said. "I'm Birdie Gaux."

Mr. Santini frowned. He turned out to be good at it! I'd never seen a better frown, not close. "Claire Gaux's granddaughter?"

"That's right."

"Hmm," said Mr. Santini. Then he muttered something that sounded like, "Influential in certain quarters for some stupid reason."

"Sorry," Birdie said. "I didn't catch that."

"Nothing," said Mr. Santini. "Is your grandma the voting type?"

"The voting type?" Birdie said.

"In elections," said Mr. Santini. "For sheriff, say. Just to pick an example out of thin air."

"I don't know," Birdie said.

Mr. Santini gave the pitchfork a shake. "Good citizens vote."

"Oh, I'm sure Grammy's a good citizen," Birdie said.

That seemed to calm Mr. Santini down a bit. "Okay, then," he said. "But you still haven't answered my question."

"What was it?" said Junior.

"A smart mouth, huh? What's your name?"

"Junior."

"Junior what? There's a million Juniors in this parish."

"Junior Tebbets."

Mr. Santini frowned one of his world-class frowns. "Wally Tebbets's boy?"

"Uh-huh."

"Your old man got a permit for that food truck of his?"

"Permit to do what?" said Junior.

"Permit to do what?" Mr. Santini's temper was back on the scene. "Think you can just roll up in a truck and start in to purveying—"

Birdie broke in. "There's a permit, Mr. Santini."

"There is?" said Junior.

"Tacked on the wall by the menu."

"What men—" Junior began, but then Birdie stepped on his foot, so quick you'd have missed it unless you kept close watch on Birdie, which I do.

"Okay, then," Mr. Santini said. "But things are slack in this town and I mean to do something about it. How we gonna compete?"

Birdie nodded like that made sense, so maybe it did. "As for your question," she said, "we're here to see Drea Bolden."

"Biker gal from New Orleans?" Mr. Santini said.

"I'm not sure she's a biker," Birdie said.

"She's on a bike, ain't she?"

"Yes, sir."

"She has green hair, don't she?"

"Partly."

"Partly is too darn much when it comes to green hair," Mr. Santini said. "What you want with her?"

"She's going to teach Junior how to read music."

Mr. Santini stroked his chin. He had hardly any chin at all—not a good human look, in my opinion. "Read music, huh? Why'd anyone want to do that?"

"It's . . . for a competition," Birdie said. "Junior's going to compete in a music-reading competition."

"I—" Junior began, but Birdie stepped on his foot again, even quicker than before.

"Competition, huh?" said Mr. Santini. "That's more like it. I guess you can't help bein' kids, huh? Same goes for the dog, maybe more so. Space ninety-six, end of Paradise Way."

We strolled down the middle path with me in the middle between Birdie and Junior. The middle of the middle! That felt comfortable, hard to explain why.

100

"My foot hurts," Junior said.

"Toughen up," said Birdie.

Junior gave her a sideways look that I caught but Birdie didn't. "Rory Cannon's a friend of yours, huh?"

"Yeah."

"He's a baseball player."

"Well, he plays baseball."

"I see them practicing on my way home from the truck. It looks so boring."

Birdie grunted.

"You like baseball?" Junior said.

"It's all right."

"You like jocks?"

"Jocks?" Birdie said.

"Like Rory Cannon," said Junior.

"I wouldn't say he's a jock."

"No? What is he?"

Birdie shrugged. "A kid."

There was a silence. We rounded a bend on Paradise Way, and the pond came into view, a murky-looking pond with lots of lily pads on the surface and a green tent set up on the near side.

"Jocks are boring," said Junior.

What was going on? I had no idea, except now it was Birdie's turn to give Junior a sidelong glance that he missed but I caught. I felt a bit uncomfortable and maybe would have done some panting, but at that moment the front flap of the green tent opened and out stepped Drea Bolden, coffee cup in hand, and the sun glinting on the bright green tips of her hair. She took a sip, then went still—the way humans sometimes do when they sense the presence of someone else—and looked our way.

"Hey, kids! Come on down!"

We went down a gentle slope—all the slopes in bayou country being gentle—and said hi to Drea, Birdie and Junior actually saying hi and me wagging my tail and then picking up an interesting scent, specifically the scent of a ham sandwich, and following it to the tent.

"So, Junior," Drea said, "you're into music."

"Music's cool," said Junior.

"And you, Birdie?" said Drea. "You into music, too?"

"Don't know about into," said Birdie. "But I like music. Some music, anyway. My great-granddaddy played the accordion."

"Yeah?" Drea said, her green eyes brightening. "Did he live long enough for you to know him?"

Birdie shook her head. "Not close."

"No? I sense a story behind that."

Birdie opened her mouth to say something, but Junior was quicker. "You want great-granddaddy stories? My great-granddaddy ran guns to both sides in the Cuban Revolution!"

Drea gazed at him for a moment, then turned back to Birdie. "You were about to say?"

"Well," said Birdie, "it's a long—"

"Hey!" Junior said. "Maybe I could write a song about gunrunning and the Cuban Revolution."

Drea's voice got a bit edgy. "Do you know much about the Cuban Revolution?"

"I've heard of it," Junior said, his voice a little muffled now, on account of the fact that I'd worked my way past an annoying tent peg or two, under the nylon skirt at the bottom of the tent, and right inside. It was dim and shadowy in the tent, but dim and shadowy never bothers me.

"Tell you what," Drea said, her voice also muffled. "Why don't I bring my guitar and some sheet music and we'll get to work?"

By that time, I'd located the ham sandwich, partly eaten and lying on a cooler. It was the work of almost no time at all to amble over to the cooler and snap up the ham sandwich, which I'd just finished doing when the flap opened and Drea came in. Her guitar lay on a sleeping bag. She picked it up, took a nail file from her pocket, and then noticed me, standing actually quite close to her, the ham sandwich in my mouth, impossible to miss.

"Well, well," said Drea. "Aren't we the sneaky ones?" Then she took the file to one of the guitar strings, back and forth, back and forth. A notch appeared in the string. Drea stopped filing before it broke.

nine

BACK OUTSIDE, DREA SAT ON A TREE stump near the edge of the pond and strapped on her guitar. Birdie and Junior sat on a log. I lay near Birdie, my energy level kind of low, which can happen to anyone on a full stomach. Out on the pond, a big frog sat on a lily pad, his throat making strange bulging motions. His eyes seemed to be on me, and the expression in them was not friendly. I wondered what to do about that.

"Here's what I'm going to play," Drea said, handing a sheet of paper to Junior. "It's just a single-note run, very simple."

"The notes are these little circles?" Junior said. Birdie leaned in to see.

"Exactly," said Drea. "The lines are the staff. And under each note I've written what it is—in this case C, G, C, C, G, etc." She ran her thumb across the strings and then began picking them one by one. At the same time, she sang, "You better come on in my kitchen, it's goin' to be rainin' outdoors."

"Hey!" Junior said.

"Wow," said Birdie. "You've got a great voice."

Drea smiled and shook her head. "Interesting, but nowhere near great."

"Huh?" said Junior. "Sounded great to me."

"Lots of color, an appealing roughness—as a music producer back in New Orleans put it, saying no in a nice way—but I don't hit the notes dead center."

"Dead center?" Junior said. "I don't get it."

"Sing," Drea said.

"Me? Like what?"

"What I just sang—I'll play along."

"You better come on in my kitchen," Junior sang, "it's goin' to be rainin' outdoors."

"Ah," Drea said. "Uh. Well . . . I . . . can see why you're a drummer. Your sense of rhythm is . . . all there is. I mean, all there. Your sense of rhythm is all there, in every note."

"Yeah?" Junior said, looking real happy.

"And how about you, Birdie?"

Birdie shook her head.

"Come on," Drea said. "Junior and I plunged right in."

Plunge right in? That was the moment I got the idea about how to handle that bothersome frog! More on that later. Now Drea started playing the tune again, and Birdie sang, softly at first and then stronger, finally tailing off at the very end.

"You better come on in my kitchen, it's goin' to be rainin' outdoors."

Things went silent down by the pond. Drea had her head tilted a bit to one side, was looking at Birdie in a new way. "Dead center," she said. "Each and every one. But with no break in the flow. And the dynamics!"

"Dynamics?" said Junior.

"Loud, soft, getting louder, getting softer, that kind of thing," Drea said. "Like so." She started strumming the guitar, first quietly, then getting louder and louder and louder, her strumming hand a blur, and—"Oops."

"Oops?" said Junior.

"I broke a string," Drea said. "See?" The broken string dangled loose. "You could do me a big favor, Junior."

"Yeah?"

"Run into town and buy me a new E string."

"Run into town? And buy it where?"

"Claymore's sell guitar strings," said Birdie.

"There you go," Drea said. She handed him some money. "And keep the change."

"Keep the change from a twenty?" said Junior. And he was off.

■ ■ ■

Drea put the guitar aside. "Funny how music runs in families," she said.

"I didn't know that," Birdie said.

"Look up the Bach family sometime."

"How do you spell that?"

Drea smiled. "B-A-C-H," she said. "Tell me about this great-grandfather of yours, the accordion player."

"He was my grammy's dad," Birdie said. "I don't know much about him. Mr. Savoy at the library has a record of him playing."

Drea gazed out at the pond. The frog was still there, eyeing me in that hostile way and doing the throat-bulging thing. "And your own dad," Drea said. "Is he musical, too?"

"My dad's dead," Birdie said. "I don't know whether he was musical or not. I was very young."

Drea kept her eyes on the pond. "Oh, I'm sorry."

"That's okay."

"Do you have any memories of him?"

"A few," Birdie said.

"Like?"

Birdie said nothing.

Drea turned to her. "My apologies, Birdie. Didn't mean to be personal. The fact is my own dad's dead, as well, so I took the liberty. Gives us something in common, although I was somewhat older than you at the time, meaning I have lots of memories."

108

"Oh," Birdie said. "Uh, I'm sorry, too."

Drea laughed. "No need. Awkward old me strikes again."

Then they just sat there for a bit, Birdie on the log, Drea on the tree stump. I found myself inching down toward the edge of the pond.

Birdie cleared her throat. "One thing I remember is these blue shoes I had, and how he tied them for me and said, 'No loose ends, Birdie.'"

Drea nodded. "A good memory to have."

"But," Birdie said.

"But what?"

Birdie was silent.

"Go ahead," Drea said, her voice very soft.

Birdie gazed in my direction, although I got the strange feeling she wasn't seeing me. "But," she said, "it's the only one. My only memory of him. So puny. Like he almost . . . wasn't real."

Drea reached out like she was going to take Birdie's hand, then stopped herself. "What did he do?" she said. "If you don't mind my asking."

Birdie's eyes went back to normal, seeing what was around in their usual way. "My dad was a detective with the New Orleans Police Department. He was killed in . . . uh, what's the expression?"

"The line of duty?"

"Yeah," Birdie said. "The line of duty. We have his medal of honor at home."

"Is that any . . . comfort at all?" said Drea. I thought I saw her eyes tear up, but by then I was too far away to be sure.

"Kind of," Birdie said.

"In a better-than-nothing sort of way?"

Birdie nodded.

"Do you know much about how it happened?" Drea said.

"He was working on a case. That's pretty much all I know."

"What kind of case?"

"Murder," Birdie said.

Drea's gaze shifted to the pond again, where I seemed to be paws deep at the moment. "Any idea who got murdered?"

"No," Birdie said.

"Or whether the case ended up getting solved?"

"I know it didn't—my grammy calls down to New Orleans every year."

"Meaning it's a cold case," said Drea.

Birdie nodded. Her mouth opened like she was going to say something, but she stayed silent.

"Go ahead," said Drea, her voice softening again, almost like faraway music.

"I just heard that expression the other day, is all," Birdie said.

"Cold case?"

"Yeah. The sheriff—Sheriff Cannon—is kind of a friend of the family. He knew my dad and mentioned something my dad once said about cold cases."

"Which was?"

Birdie licked her lips. " 'You warm up cold cases by caring about the survivors.' "

Now there were tears in Drea's eyes, no question. Even from where I was by then—out in the pond, pretty much up to my chest—I could see those tears, wobbling bubbles in the sun. Too big and wobbly not to overflow, which they did. Drea dabbed at her cheeks with the back of her hand.

"Is something wrong?" Birdie said.

Now Drea did reach for Birdie's hand. She took it in her own. "We're survivors, you and me."

Birdie gazed down at their two hands together. Drea was watching Birdie's face. Things felt peaceful down at Mr. Santini's pond. That was around when my paws stopped touching the bottom and I went from walking to swimming.

Meanwhile, Drea had let go of Birdie's hand. "Ever heard of *Kramer's Kold Kases*?"

"No," Birdie said. "What is it?"

"A blog," said Drea. "All Ks where the Cs should be."

"What about it?"

"There's a lot of crazy stuff online. But . . . but not all of it, right?"

"I don't know," Birdie said.

Ah, swimming! Swimming is simply trotting underwater. What could be better than that? How about swimming directly at an annoying frog poised on a lily pad that was now real close by? What a life I was living! The frog gazed at me like I was a nobody, throat bulging in that annoying way. Get ready for some big life changes, Mr. Frog.

Meanwhile, from the shore, still well within range of hearing like mine, I heard more talk. Birdie said, "What happened to your dad?"

Before Drea could answer, I was distracted by a bright glare on the far side of the pond. I looked that way and saw a man, mostly hidden by a tree trunk, watching us through binoculars. More accurately, from how the binoculars were pointing, the man was watching Birdie and Drea. That bothered me. Then I noticed the man's hair—thick, golden, puffy. And his mustache, somewhat darker. Had I seen this man before? Oh, yes, driving slowly down Gentilly Lane in a sporty two-seater, a cat with a coat similar in color to the man's golden dome curled up on the back shelf. That bothered me some more. I barked, a very loud and sharp bark I have for when sneaky things are going on.

That bark got everyone's attention. The frog turned out to have the fastest reaction time, springing off the lily pad and disappearing beneath the scummy surface of the pond. The man was second-fastest, darting into the trees on the far side and vanishing from sight. Then came Birdie. "Bowser? What is it? What's going on?"

"Could there be gators in this pond?" Drea said.

"Bowser can smell them," Birdie said. "He wouldn't go in."

Wow! Was that true? I felt very good about myself, although this was not the time for too much of that, not with the man running away through the trees. I barked louder and sharper.

"Are you sure?" Drea said.

"Yes," Birdie said. "But—Bowser, come!"

Come? Now? With the golden-domed dude running away? I didn't like him, not one little bit, and—

"Bowser! Come! Treat!"

Treat? That was another story. I left off with the barking for the time being and swam for shore. Moments later I was munching on a tasty biscuit, the annoying frog and the golden-domed dude with the binoculars fading fast

113

from my mind. We walked back to the tent, Drea on one side of me, Birdie on the other. Drea glanced over my head at Birdie.

"Ever hear of people named Richelieu around here?" she said.

"Yeah," said Birdie. "They were the other ones who got broken into."

Drea stopped in her tracks. "Broken into? I don't understand."

Birdie got started on a long explanation about the break-ins and how nothing got taken from either place, including Mrs. Richelieu's pearls—even if no one knew the truth about that, the whole story just about impossible to follow.

"The truth about her pearls?" said Drea. "What do you mean?"

"Well," Birdie began, and then she paused and looked at Drea from a different angle, her head tilted to the side. "Wait a minute," she said. "Were you looking for the Richelieus this morning? When we met on the bridge?"

"Why would you think that?"

"Because it was their boat—*Cardinal*—that had just gone through," Birdie said. "And you asked if we'd seen a boat, me and Junior."

"Speak of the devil," Drea said. And at that moment,

Junior came running up with a small package in his hand. "To be continued," Drea said softly, like she was talking to herself.

"Grade A guitar strings," Junior said. "Same kind as used by ZZ Top, whoever he is. Says right on 'em."

"Thanks, Junior," Drea said, taking the package from him. She checked her watch. "But I've got to be somewhere. How about we meet here tomorrow, same time?"

"Uh, sure," Junior said. "Did Birdie tell you about 'Stay Away, Friend'?"

"What's that?" said Drea.

"My very latest song."

"Something to look forward to," Drea said.

Rory was standing outside our house when we got home. He was all sweaty and dusty, wore his baseball uniform, carried a bat over his shoulder, a baseball glove slung on the tip of the barrel. A leather baseball glove with rawhide laces: By far the most interesting object I'd run across in some time.

"There you are," he said.

"Hi," said Birdie.

"I knocked but no one answered."

"No one's home."

"You're home now."

"Right."

"Had a game today. Second-last game of the season."

"How'd it go?"

"Oh-for-two. Only had two at bats on account of the slaughter rule."

"Who got slaughtered?" Birdie said. "You or them?"

"Us," said Rory. He looked down at the grass, kind of . . . pawed at it with one of his cleats. I couldn't help liking Rory. "I think I'm seeing the ball, but maybe I'm not."

"Oh," Birdie said.

Rory looked up. "Oh? Just oh?"

"It's only a game, Rory."

"I hate when people say that."

Uh-oh. They weren't getting along? I paused what I'd been doing, namely getting myself in position to spring up and make a play for that glove hanging off the end of the bat.

"But maybe thinking about it like that would help you relax," Birdie said.

Rory raised his voice. "I am relaxed!"

"Good to hear," said Birdie.

Rory glared at her. "I came to tell you something."

"What?"

"You've been hanging out with Junior Tebbets, huh?"

"That's what you came to tell me?"

Rory shook his head real fast and hard, like he was trying to shake things up in there. "Forget I said that." He wiped his sweaty face with the back of his hand, leaving a reddish smear on his cheek, the color of the base paths down at the ball fields.

"Okay," Birdie said.

"What I came to tell you was about the pearls."

"What about them?"

"The pearls that got stolen from the Richelieus, that no one's supposed to know about."

"Go on."

"You haven't told anybody?"

"Of course not."

"The thing is," Rory said, "they're worth a lot of money. Mrs. Richelieu put in a claim to her insurance company and they called my dad, which is how come I overheard, like on the police line in the kitchen. See what I'm saying? It's kind of complicated."

"How much?" Birdie said.

"Huh?"

"How much are—were—the pearls worth?"

"Twenty thousand dollars," Rory said.

"Wow," said Birdie.

Were they getting along better now? I thought so, and

picked up where I'd left off, inching my way into position. I could practically taste those rawhide laces, rawhide being one of the tastiest things out there.

"Why's Bowser creeping along on his belly like that?" Rory said.

Birdie gave me a close look. "Don't even think about it," she said. "Meaning you, Bowser."

Me? Suddenly I was center stage? I stopped what I was doing, opened my mouth wide and let my tongue flap way, way out. It was all I could think to do.

"Maybe we can catch them on the way back in," Birdie said, opening a kitchen drawer and taking out a small black camera.

Sounded like a plan to me, although I had no idea what she was talking about. Did Birdie ever go wrong? That thought didn't even make sense. Next thing I knew we were out the door, and not long after that we were back on the Lucinda Street Bridge. The sun was lower in the sky now and everything looked different from before, the bayou no longer blue, but a kind of red gold, crisscrossed with the long shadows of trees that grew on the banks. Birdie watched in silence, those shadows growing longer and longer.

"You see the plan, Bowser?" she said.

And of course I did. My plan was to stay here on the bridge with Birdie for as long as she wanted.

"The sheriff needs to know those pearls weren't stolen," Birdie went on. "But he has to find out in a way that doesn't lead back to Rory. So what if a time-stamped photo of Mrs. Richelieu with the pearls shows up in his mail?"

Sounded good to me, whatever it was. I was familiar with mailboxes, of course, had marked just about every one of them in town.

Birdie gazed down the bayou. Were we waiting for something? I got that impression, but couldn't think what. After a while I heard engine sounds on the way. Right around then was when Birdie sighed. "I guess we're too late, Bowser. We'll have to come up with another idea."

Too late? Too late for what? She couldn't mean too late for a boat, because one would clearly be along in no time. Or was it possible she wasn't picking up those engine sounds, practically a din by now? I stared at her ears and felt bad for her.

"Let's go," she said.

Which was just when a boat rounded a bend down the bayou and came into view. Birdie was already taking a first step or two the other way, headed off the bridge. I barked a low rumbly bark, just making myself useful.

Birdie stopped, turned, looked in the direction I wanted her to look.

"Good boy," she said, taking out the camera.

My tail started up in a cheerful way, unfortunately knocking the camera from Birdie's hand. It bounced across the pavement, skittered to the very edge of the bridge and—and came to rest right there. Birdie scooped it up, so no harm, no foul.

The boat turned out to be a boat I'd seen before, namely the cabin cruiser that belonged to the Richelieus, red with black trim. *Cardinal*, if I was remembering right— something you shouldn't count on for one second. It was still pretty far away. Miranda stood at the controls, at this distance her face just a shape with no features. No sign of Merv. Birdie leaned over the rail, peering into the camera.

"Too far away to see much, Bowser. Maybe if I turn this gizmo, I'll be able to—oh my god! She's wearing them!"

Birdie snapped a picture. At that moment, Merv came out of the cabin and approached Miranda. He waved something at her. A purse? Maybe. Then they seemed to have a conversation, brief but unpleasant. Miranda took something off her neck. The pearls? Had to be. She dropped them into the purse. Merv took the purse into the cabin. *Cardinal* came chugging toward the bridge.

120

"Let's go, Bowser!"

We started off the bridge and were almost on the street when Miranda looked up and saw us. Her eyes opened wide. Dark and unfriendly eyes, and real smart. They found the camera in Birdie's hand right away. *Cardinal* glided under the bridge and out of sight.

ten

WE WALKED OFF THE LUCINDA STREET
Bridge, Birdie moving so fast I had to trot
to keep up with her. Were we in a hurry?
I didn't know and didn't care, speed always a good thing,
in my opinion. Speed clears your mind like nothing else!
We crossed the street, Birdie glancing back when we
reached the other side. *Cardinal* was somewhat distant
now, motoring slowly up the bayou, more like a dark
shadow in the low light.

"Do you think she recognized us?" Birdie said. "She
scares me, Bowser."

Who were we talking about? I waited to find out but
Birdie didn't say.

Grammy was setting the table in the kitchen when we
got home.

"Something smells good," Birdie said, sniffing the air
with her puny nose. What a great kid! As for the smells,
where to actually begin breaking them down? It would
take forever.

122

"Crawfish casserole," Grammy said.

"I love your crawfish casserole!" Birdie said, watching Grammy lay down some plates. "Four places, Grammy?"

"Uh-huh," said Grammy.

"Who's the fourth?"

The only thought that came to me was: Hey! Ol' Bowser's sitting at the table tonight! But I'm not at my best with numbers, so I knew not to get my hopes up. The problem is that my hopes are always just sitting there waiting to get way, way up, like balloons. How do you keep balloons from happening?

"Some work contact your mama's bringing for dinner," Grammy said. "There was a meeting for everybody who got fired." Grammy gave Birdie a close look. "What are you doing with that camera?"

"Um," said Birdie, glancing down at the camera in her hand like it was a surprise. "Taking some pictures."

"Pictures? What pictures?"

"You know. Pictures of stuff."

"Stuff?"

"Stuff around town," Birdie said.

"Stuff around town, huh?" said Grammy. "School can't start up too soon."

We went into Mama's room. Mama had a printer at her desk. Birdie got busy with the camera and the printer, and soon held up a sheet of paper. "Not a very good picture, Bowser, but those pearls are clear and on her neck and that's what counts. Plus there's the date stamp." She folded the sheet of paper, stuck it in an envelope, found a pen. "How about"—she started writing on the envelope—"Sheriff Cannon, Police Station, St. Roch, Louisiana?"

Sounded good to me. Birdie licked the envelope and right away that was something I wanted to be doing, too. But before I could take even one step in that direction, Birdie had tucked the envelope under her T-shirt, out of my range. We left Mama's room, went through the kitchen—

"Where you going now, child?"

"Be right back, Grammy!"

—and out the door. A blue box stood a few doors down on the other side of the street. Birdie dropped the envelope inside.

Birdie helped Grammy finish setting the table. I went to the corner by the fridge and lapped up some water from my bowl. Grammy checked her watch. I heard a car pulling into the driveway—Mama's car, which I knew from a little *tick-tick-tick* sound it made—and just after that another car stopped out front, on the street. Car doors closed, *thump-thump*, and then came footsteps on the walk and onto the breezeway, two sets of footsteps, Mama's and those of some man.

The door opened and in walked Mama, carrying some folders. Behind her came a man, a bottle of wine in his hand and a smile on his face. The smell of limey aftershave flowed into our kitchen. The hair on my neck—on my whole back, all the way to the tip of my tail—went stiff, stiff like rows of iron spikes.

"Grammy," Mama said, "I'd like you to meet Mr. Pardo."

"Vin, please," said Mr. Pardo.

"Vin," Mama went on, "this is my mother-in-law, Claire Gaux."

Grammy gave him a little nod. "Nice to meet you."

"The pleasure's all mine, ma'am," said Vin Pardo.

"And this is my daughter, Birdie."

"What a great name! Hi, Birdie."

A growling started up in our kitchen, not loud, but as fierce as you'd ever want to hear.

"Hi, Mr. Pardo," Birdie said.

"Vin was at the meeting," Mama said.

"You work at the company, too?" said Grammy.

"No, ma'am," said Vin Pardo. "But when word gets out that a lot of talented folks are suddenly available, I come runnin'."

"You're a competitor?" said Grammy.

"Not exactly," said Vin Pardo. "I'm in—" He broke off, turned to me. "But who's this handsome fella? He doesn't appear to like me much."

By this time, I'd narrowed the gap between me and Pardo, down to the distance of an easy lunge.

"This is Bowser," Mama said. "And I'm sure he likes you."

Mama was wrong about that, as wrong as wrong could be. Where to begin? First of all, Vin Pardo was no stranger to me. I'd seen him driving slowly past our house in that sporty two-seater, seen him again watching Birdie and Drea through binoculars from across the scummy pond at Santini's Campground. And that wasn't all! After the break-in hadn't I smelled limey aftershave all through the house? Now limey aftershave was back, back big-time. All that was new about this man with the thin, dark mustache and the puffy dome of golden hair was his name.

Pardo laughed. "He sure has a funny way of showing it."

"Bowser," Birdie hissed. "Stop that growling."

Growling? Yes, that was me, and for a good reason. Growling was the way to go at times like this, possibly even followed by biting. I amped it up. Pardo laughed harder. That was too much!

"Bowser!" Birdie said.

126

But by that time I had him! An easy lunge? Even easier than I'd thought. Oh, yeah! I sank my teeth deep into Pardo's leg, and if not his leg—on account of him dodging away with surprising speed—then at least clear through the fabric of his trousers. Then came lots of commotion, possibly including a cry of fear from Pardo, followed by the sudden grip of a very strong hand on my collar. The strong hand turned out to be Mama's. She whisked me across the kitchen, out into the hall, and slammed the door practically right in my face. First I thought: Bowser the hero, strikes again! My second thought was: What had I done?

Voices came through the door.

Mama: "Vin, I'm so sorry."

Grammy: "Disgraceful!"

Birdie: "I'm sure he didn't mean it. He's never done anything like that before."

Grammy: "Once is more than enough."

Mama: "I can sew up that tear in a jiffy."

Pardo: "No problem. Please don't go to any trouble on my account. And . . . and what I'm guessing this is all about is him smelling cat on me."

Did I smell cat on him? Of course! But it wasn't that. At least, not only that. I clawed at the door.

Mama: "Bowser!"

Grammy: "Bowser!"

Birdie: "Bowser, please."

I started amping it down. Somehow Birdie, Mama, and Grammy—my people!—were alone with Vin Pardo. Who was in charge of security at 19 Gentilly Lane? Wouldn't that be me? Therefore, it was my duty to keep Pardo in sight. I turned my voice into what you might call a pleasant murmur.

Birdie: "He's whimpering."

Grammy: "I'll give him something to whimper about."

Birdie: "He'll be good. I promise."

Mama: "Vin?"

Pardo: "Fine with me. Just give me a moment to get up on the table."

Lots of laughter followed that, and then the door opened. Birdie gave me a—oh, no!—sort of sternish look. "Go right to your bowl and lie down."

I trotted in a straight line over to my water bowl in the corner and lay down, paws tucked underneath, eyes on nobody. Pardo got up and came over.

"Bowser," Birdie said, "you be good."

Pardo bent down and said, "Let's be friends." He patted my head, just a little too hard. The look he gave me—there and gone real quick—was not the least bit friendly. I closed my eyes. Pardo straightened. "Back on track with man's best friend," he said.

More laughter. "So you've got a cat?" Mama said.

"She's got me, more like it," said Pardo.

Mama laughed some more. I opened my eyes, and happened to notice Grammy watching Mama laugh, watching closely, Grammy-style. "What's her name?" Mama said.

"Bonnie," Pardo said.

"Like in Bonnie and Clyde?" said Grammy.

Pardo smiled at her. "I just like the name," he said. He went over to Grammy, handed her the bottle of wine. "So nice of you to invite me into your home."

"You're welcome," said Grammy.

"Did I just hear there's a whole other wing?"

"Wouldn't call it a wing," Grammy said. "More like a separate apartment, actually, across the breezeway."

Pardo glanced at the door that led to the breezeway. "Ah," he said.

"Crawfish casserole?" Pardo said as Grammy spooned some on his plate. "This is my lucky day." He raised his glass. "Here's to the Gaux."

"No stopping us," said Grammy.

"Ha!" said Pardo. "That's funny."

He took a sip of wine. So did Grammy—just a small one. Mama had what looked to me, over in the corner by my bowl, like a pretty big gulp. Birdie had a big gulp, too, but she was drinking water.

Pardo tried the crawfish casserole. "Mmm. Delicious. Don't suppose you'd share the recipe."

"Sure," said Grammy. "Right out of Betty Crocker. Does your wife like to cook?"

"No wife," Pardo said, looking down for a moment like he was having an unhappy spell. "I'm divorced."

"Kids?" said Grammy.

"None."

"Ah," Grammy said.

Pardo looked up, the dark mood, if that's what it had been, quickly shaken off. "But this sure has the feel of a happy home."

"Thanks," said Mama, reaching for her wineglass.

"So, Mr. Pardo," Grammy began.

"Vin, please," said Pardo.

"So you're not with Jen's company?"

Mama's name was Jen? I was just finding that out now? Or . . . or she had more than one name? What sense did that make? For example, I was Bowser, period. So what was going on with—

Birdie turned to me, her eyes—alarmed, you might say. "Shh." Had a growl started up again? I wasn't sure, but made an effort to get a grip on any growling that might have involved me. I'm a team player, probably not news to you by this time.

"No, ma'am," Pardo said, wiping his mouth on the napkin, but missing a tiny casserole scrap that had stuck in his mustache. "I run a little operation down in New Orleans."

"An operation in the oil patch?" Grammy said.

"Not exclusively," Pardo said. "I'm an investor—maybe that's the best way to put it. Always on the lookout for trends. The details are probably kind of boring."

"I'm not bored," Grammy said. "But I don't want to be prying."

Mama spoke up, maybe a little on the loud side. "Especially when we can google him later."

Grammy's eyebrows rose, and so did Birdie's.

Pardo laughed. "Let me know what you find out, Jen," he said. "In the meantime, just shoot me your résumé and I'll draw up a list of possible matches. We can go over them and if you give the go-ahead I'll make some calls."

"That's so kind of you," Mama said.

"Just good business," Pardo said. "Got to give before you take—that's what investing is. I try to apply that idea in everyday life."

"Well," said Grammy, sipping her wine. "Well, well, well."

"But enough about me," Pardo said. "I get the feeling I've stumbled upon one of those famous clans you hear about from up in these parts. Tell me about the Gaux."

"Clans?" Grammy said. "I wouldn't know about that."

"Sorry if I misspoke," said Pardo. "How about strong, multigenerational families?"

"No denying that, Grammy," said Mama.

"What's 'multigenerational'?" said Birdie.

"Just like this," Mama said. "Grandmother, mother, and daughter, all together."

Pardo nodded. "Very nice, the way you put that," he said. "Even—" At that point, maybe jarred loose by the nodding, the little scrap of casserole fell from Pardo's mustache and splashed down—with a tiny splash—in Pardo's wineglass. His smile faded and he gave that little scrap—now sinking to the bottom of glass—a real annoyed look. But the look vanished so fast I ended up not being sure I'd really seen it. Sometimes I imagine things. Once, for example, I imagined that I could get into the fridge just by clawing at it. Let's not bother with what happened after that.

"Even," Pardo went on, giving Mama a little smile, "even touching. How long have you all lived in St. Roch?"

"Grammy's people have been here since . . . since when, Grammy?" Mama said. "Going way back, I know that."

"Seventeen eighty-five, according to tradition," Grammy said. "But there's no proof."

"Happy to take your word for it, ma'am," Pardo said, raising his glass to Grammy. He gazed into it for a moment, swirled it around. "And you, Jen?" he said. "If you're the daughter-in-law you must have married into the family."

"That's right," Mama said. "I married—was so very fortunate to marry—Claire's son, Robert."

Pardo glanced around the room. Looking for what? I had no idea.

"Who," Mama went on, "is no longer with us."

"Meaning dead," said Grammy.

"Oh, I'm sorry," Pardo said. "I had no intention of—"

"Nothing for you to be sorry about," Grammy said. "You didn't do it."

At that moment, Pardo came close to dropping his wine-glass. It actually did slip from his fingers, but he caught it almost immediately, a big golden wave of wine slopping over the top of the glass. He grabbed his napkin, took some stabs at mopping up.

"Good god," he said, "so clumsy of me. Please forgive—"

"No harm done," Mama said, reaching for the bottle and topping up his glass. "It's just a little wine."

"I'm happy to have the tablecloth laundered," Pardo said. "Or even better, I'll send you a replacement."

"Don't be silly," said Grammy. "And besides, it's white wine. White wine don't stain. It's the red you can't get out."

Pardo licked his lips, then licked them again. He had a whitish tongue, and kind of pointy. "Baking soda," he said, but it was more of a thick, low mutter, as though something was clogged inside.

"Beg pardon?" Grammy said.

Pardo cleared his throat, took a big swallow from his glass. "Baking soda, ma'am," he said. "Baking soda does the trick on red wine."

"Much obliged," said Grammy. "I'll remember that."

"And now, Vin," Mama said, "let's hear a little more about you."

"Not much to tell really." He cleared his throat again, gave his head a little shake, as though getting inside-the-head things back in order. "Born in New Orleans, only child, parents divorced, ended up on my own pretty young, got involved with one thing and another, mostly in construction, lucked into an ownership stake, got bought out at the right time, used the proceeds to get into real estate, lucked out there as well. So now"—he smiled at Mama—"I am where I am."

"Well, well," Grammy said. "And what's the name of this company of yours?"

"Bonnie Investments," Pardo said.

"Named after your cat?" said Grammy.

"Yup."

"That's funny," Mama said.

"I thought so," said Pardo, giving her another smile.

I myself saw nothing funny about Bonnie the cat, or anything named after her. Or about anything going on in our kitchen, for that matter. But I stayed by my bowl, a threat to no one. From there I could see that the above-the-tabletop part of Vin Pardo was nice and relaxed, but down underneath one of his legs was going a mile a minute, which I'm guessing is pretty fast.

eleven

ELICIOUS," SAID VIN PARDO, DOWNING his last bite of pecan pie. "You should open a restaurant, Claire."

"Fastest way to lose money yet invented," Grammy said.

"You're right about that," Pardo said. "Based on that exact same insight, I once bought a restaurant equipment supplier."

"Figuring that the turnover in restaurants would drive up demand?" Mama said.

Pardo pointed his fork at Mama. "See, right there is why you're going to have your pick of good jobs in no time flat."

Mama's face pinkened a bit.

"So the restaurant supply company made money?" Grammy said.

"Actually, no," said Pardo. "Turns out that the restaurant supply business is the second-fastest money loser known to man. But that doesn't change Jen's prospects, not one bit. It's the presentation that counts."

"I don't quite understand," Mama said.

"It's all about communication," Pardo said, wiping his mouth with his napkin and pushing back his chair. He looked around the kitchen. "What a great space!"

"This kitchen?" Grammy said. "What's great about it?"

"Hard to put in words," Pardo said. "And I'm no architect. Just a plain ol' businessman. But tell you what—I sure would appreciate a quick tour."

"A tour of the house?" Grammy said. "What in heaven's name for?"

"Just a little idea germinating in my mind," said Pardo. "But if it's any trouble at all, the last thing I'd want to do is—"

"It's no trouble," Mama said, pushing back her own chair, as though maybe she was about to show Pardo around our place.

But before that could happen—or Mama could say another word—Grammy spoke up. "Birdie," she said. "Show Mr. Pardo around."

"Vin, please," Pardo said.

"Me?" said Birdie.

"Either that or the washing up," Grammy said.

Pardo laughed. Mama shot Grammy a quick glance and then sort of laughed, too. Sometimes, hanging around with humans, you get the strange feeling you're missing the whole show. I was having that feeling now.

"Can Bowser come?" Birdie said.

"Well," Mama began.

"Of course the little fella can come," Pardo said, waving me over. "Now that we're buds."

"Come, Bowser," Birdie said.

Little fella? Had to do my best to ignore that. I rose and trotted across the room, stood close to Birdie. And rock solidly between her and Pardo.

"Where should I start?" Birdie said.

Mama shrugged. "There's really not that much to see. Maybe start with the living room, then a quick peek into the bedrooms, I suppose, and out the side door and round to the back."

"Okay," Birdie said, and headed toward the hallway. Pardo followed her. I followed Pardo, kept him right in front of me. The backs of human legs can feel nervous, as you probably know already. The backs of Pardo's legs were nervous at the moment. My mood brightened. From behind came the sound of water running in the sink.

"Well," Birdie said, "this here's the living room."

"Uh-huh," said Pardo.

"That's the TV and there's Bowser's bed for napping in the daytime."

Pardo glanced back at me. "Does he go everywhere you go?"

"Pretty much," said Birdie. "Anything else you'd like to see in the living room?"

"No."

We headed down the hall.

"Mama's room."

"Nice and tidy."

"My room. Mine and Bowser's."

"Love the walls—just like the sky. And hey! You've got a nifty little camera. Take many pictures?"

"Not really."

"Mind if I check it out? Happen to be in the market for a new camera myself."

"Uh, sure." Birdie went to the desk, got the camera, handed it to Pardo.

"How about we snap one of Bowser?" He pointed the camera at me, did some fiddling with it, then some more fiddling, paused for what seemed like a longish moment and said, "Smile." After that came a click, and next he was showing the picture he'd taken to Birdie. "He's one photogenic dog," Pardo said.

"Thanks," said Birdie. She put the camera back on the desk, and the tour continued, meaning pretty soon we came to the end, 19 Gentilly Lane not being what you'd call a mansion—like the Richelieus' place, for example.

"Here's the side door," Birdie said.

"Got time to show me the yard?"

"Sure."

We went outside. It was almost dark now, except for a dull reddish band down at the very bottom of one part of the sky. Birdie switched on the outside light and we walked around to the backyard.

"Here's the picnic table, Mr. Pardo." Birdie said.

"It's Vin."

"Oh, sorry."

"No problem." Pardo flashed a quick smile, but his eyes were on the breezeway, specifically the door to Grammy's part of the house.

"And here's the carport," Birdie said, switching on the carport lights. Under the carport roof, a few outboard motors rested on a wooden stand. "Grammy fixes these up." Birdie picked up a screwdriver that had fallen to the cement floor and placed it on the stand. "She's teaching me."

Pardo shot her a glance. "You enjoy that sort of thing? Working on engines?"

"Well," said Birdie, "I'm just learning." She moved on. "And this is the breezeway and here's the door to take us back into the kitchen." She looked up at Pardo, waiting for him to say something. The breeze flowed through the breezeway, which was what breezeways were all about—it had taken me some time to nail that down—and brought his smell to me: limey aftershave, yes, but also plenty of human sweat, the sharp and nervous kind. At the same time, I could also make out the scent, faint now, but not gone, of snake. Snake under the breezeway. So much to keep track of when you're in charge of security. But a job's a job. Doing it right is what counts. What was the right thing to do about that snake? I waited for an idea to come.

"What about the other half?" Pardo said.

"Grammy's side?" said Birdie.

"While we're at it."

Birdie seemed to think about that. Then she shrugged, opened Grammy's door, switched on the lights.

"Grammy's living room. And this is her kitchen, just a little one—Grammy hardly ever eats here."

Pardo nodded. "Old people don't eat much."

"It's not that," Birdie said. "We all eat together, in the big kitchen." Birdie led us down the hall. The light threw shadows along the wall: a small one, a big one, and a four-legged one. The four-legged one was a real tough customer. If you looked carefully, you could see the tufted bits of shadow where the fur on the back of his neck was sticking up.

The door to Grammy's bedroom was open. Pardo stuck his head inside. I heard a click from somewhere in the walls, and cold air began to flow.

"What's that sound?" Pardo said, cocking his ear.

"I don't hear anything," Birdie said.

"A kind of fluttering."

Which I heard, too, goes without mentioning.

"Oh, that," Birdie said. "Grammy thinks there must be something caught in the vent."

"What vent?" Pardo said.

Birdie pointed out the grate in the ceiling.

"Ah," said Pardo. He looked down at Birdie. I moved into easy-lunging range. Pardo backed up a step or two. "Thanks for the tour—you're an excellent guide, Birdie."

"You're welcome, Mr. Pardo," Birdie said.

"Vin."

We got up bright and early the next morning, me and Birdie, and—

"Bowser, I'm so tired. Let me sleep!" She pulled the covers up to her chin. I loved that game, and pulled them right back down. "Bowser!" She pulled them up. I pulled them down. She pulled them up. I pulled them down, down and right off the bed, springing one of my best moves on her.

—and . . . and where was I? A walk. Right. We got up bright and early and went for a nice walk. Birdie didn't look the least bit tired to me. In fact, she looked just great, her hair all over the place, sleepy seeds in the corners of her eyes, her face sort of puffy, and a faint line across her cheek where the edge of the sheet had rested. Birdie was the most beautiful human on the planet, no debate about that. I marked a bush here and a hydrant there— very important to lay your own mark on top of all the others—and felt like life couldn't be better. We went through the center of town, passed the library, and came to a low brick building.

"That's my school, Bowser. It starts soon. You'll have to entertain yourself while I'm gone." She gazed down at me. "Think you can do that? I'm a little worried about it."

Birdie was worried? About me? I never wanted that to happen, not for a single second, which I'm guessing is a very short time. I went right up to the front steps of the school, if that's what this brick building was, and marked them but good. Birdie had nothing to worry about, not from me!

"Oh, Bowser!" Birdie gazed at the steps, kind of damp at the moment, and then started laughing. "Sometimes I'd like to do that to the school myself! But don't tell anybody."

Birdie's secrets were safe with me.

We went around to the fields behind the building. In the distance was a baseball diamond with a chain-link backstop. There was no one around except one kid, tossing a ball in the air and then hitting it at the backstop with his bat, at least some of the time. Mostly he swung and missed.

"Rory?" Birdie said when we got closer.

He turned to us. "I was just looking for you," he said.

"You were?"

"I was thinking of it, anyways."

We crossed the infield, reached the backstop.

"What are you doing?" Birdie said.

"The thing you told me," Rory said. "Tryin' to, is more like it."

"What did I tell you?"

"Don't you remember? To relax. Watch this." He held the bat with one hand, resting the barrel on his shoulder. With his other hand, he gave the ball a gentle toss straight up in the air, then got that hand quickly on the bat, raised the barrel off his shoulder, hurried the bat back into cocked position, and took a big swing at the ball.

And missed. The ball bounced in the dirt once or twice and came to rest against Rory's foot. I picked it up, which is what I do with balls. Baseballs were my favorite. Given time, I could gnaw my way into their insides, where things got really interesting. I was thinking, *What's wrong with now?* when Birdie stooped down and gently took possession of the ball.

144

Meanwhile, Rory was glaring at her.

"See?" he said.

"See what?" said Birdie.

"It didn't work."

"What didn't work?"

"Relaxing. In my head I was saying *relax, relax, relax*, and look what happened. I whiffed!"

"Do you think saying *relax, relax, relax* in your head is relaxing?"

"I guess not, but—"

"And there's no point in being angry at me."

Rory looked down. "Sorry, Birdie."

Birdie gazed at him. "Do you even like baseball, Rory?"

His eyes opened wide. "Do I like baseball?"

"Yeah."

"That's what you're asking me?"

"Yeah."

"So . . ." Rory shook his head. "So you don't even know me."

"Huh?"

"Asking a question like that. Baseball is . . . I don't know. Everything. And I suck at it."

Birdie put her hands on her hips. Then she blew a little puff of air through her lips, making a soft vibrating sound.

"How about I throw you some BP?" she said.

"BP?"

"Batting practice," said Birdie.

"I know what BP is! I meant, like, you?"

"Why not me?"

"You don't play baseball, for one thing," Rory said.

"I'm not playing baseball," Birdie said, giving Rory a look I'd never want her to turn on me. "I'm throwing BP. Yes or no?"

"Um, yeah, sure, I guess."

Birdie strode to the mound, baseball in hand. I followed close behind, in fact as close as close could be.

"Who's gonna catch?" Rory said.

"Bowser," said Birdie. "Bowser will catch."

"From there?"

"You'll see. Get in the batter's box."

Rory stepped into the batter's box, took his stance. Birdie's eyes narrowed down to two slits of blue sky, sort of beautiful and scary at the same time. "What's with your hands?" she said.

"What about them?"

"Shouldn't they be higher?"

"Why do you say that?"

"I saw a show about Ted Williams. His hands were up higher."

"Who's Ted Williams?"

"Never mind. Just get them higher."

Rory raised his hands. Birdie went into her windup, reared back and threw the baseball. Rory swung the bat but the ball was already by him.

"Hey! You've got a good arm!"

Birdie ignored him. "Bowser," she said. "Fetch."

Fetch? Maybe the best human invention out there. I raced to the backstop, scooped up the ball, and roared on back to the mound, offering the ball up to Birdie. She wiped it on her shorts, started into her windup.

"Whoa!" Rory said. "How come you can pitch?"

"Hands up higher," Birdie said. And then the ball was on the way. Rory swung a little quicker this time, didn't miss by as much.

"Bowser. Fetch."

But I was already there, and practically halfway back to the mound. Birdie took the ball, wiped it off, gave me a nice pat. "You're a natural-born superstar catcher, Bowser." She straightened up, gazed in at Rory. "That's better," she said.

"What is?"

"Your hands."

Rory glanced up at his hands. "Yeah? I wasn't even thinking about them."

"Don't think," Birdie said. "Don't think about anything."

"Don't think about anything?"

"That's the secret."

Wow! The secret was to not think about anything? I'd known it practically my whole life!

"Here we go," Birdie said, and she threw another pitch. Rory swung and—*CRACK*. Well, maybe just *crack*, but he got the bat on the ball, which flew on a line out to the grass beyond the basepaths. "Clean single to right," Birdie said.

"Hey! That's the first solid contact I've made in—"

"Just shut up and play." As for me, I was already back, delivering the ball. Ol' Bowser, natural-born superstar catcher. "Batter up," Birdie said.

Crack.

Fetch.

Crack.

Fetch.

CRACK!

"More like it," Birdie said.

We walked home, me in the middle, Birdie and Rory on either side. It was getting hot and their faces were pink, especially Rory's. Rory had the bat and his glove. I had the ball.

"How come you don't play sports?" he said.

"Fishing's a sport," said Birdie.

"Yeah, but I meant soccer, basketball, that kind of thing."

"Those are after school," Birdie said. "I help out at the store after school."

"Oh," said Rory. "Too bad."

"I don't think it's too bad," Birdie said. "And I like fishing."

We walked in silence for a while.

"Then how come you know how to pitch?" Rory said.

"I used to play catch."

"Yeah? Who with?"

"Grammy."

"Your grandmother plays catch?"

"Not anymore. When I was little. When she was young she used to strike out grown men for money."

"Huh?"

"At the parish fair in Houma. You paid a dollar. If you got a hit you won a stuffed bear. No one ever won a stuffed bear off Grammy."

Rory gave Birdie a look. Her eyes were straight ahead so she didn't see it, but I did. It was a real interesting look in a way I can't explain.

We came to a corner. "Guess I'll head home," Rory said. "Um, thanks."

"No problem."

"Think I could have my ball back?"

"Bowser?" Birdie said.

She wanted on opinion? On whether Rory could have the ball? That was an easy one. No. I backed away, the ball clenched firmly between my jaws, powerful jaws in case I haven't made that clear.

"It's kind of gunked up, anyway," Rory said.

Gunked up? I had no idea what he was talking about.

Rory went off one way, and we went off the other, the baseball in our custody. The day was a total win so far. But Rory hadn't gone far before he stopped and turned. I got a tight grip on the ball.

He raised his voice. "Hey!"

We stopped, too. "What?" Birdie said.

"Remember when I said I was looking for you?"

"You said you were thinking of looking for me."

"Right," Rory called. "On account of I had something to tell you."

"What about?"

"The pearls."

Birdie's eyes opened wide. "What did you say?"

Rory cupped his hands to his mouth and shouted, "The pearls!" A woman across the street, wearing a bandanna and trimming a hedge, looked our way.

"I heard you the first time," Birdie said in a sort of loud whisper. We moved quickly toward Rory. "What about the pearls?" she said, keeping her voice low.

"They turned up," Rory said.

"Shh. Turned up?"

Rory nodded. "Mrs. Richelieu called my dad first thing this morning. She found them in her laundry hamper."

twelve

WE'VE GOT A BIG PROBLEM, BOWSER," Birdie said as we walked back through the center of town.

What a surprise! I'd never have guessed we had a problem of any size, not with all the fun we'd had so far, and the day still young.

"Mrs. Richelieu's pearls were never gone, which of course we knew already, meaning you and me."

Wow! I'd known that? What a brain I was turning out to be! Totally unexpected and not even necessary, icing on the cake. Although I'm no expert on cake, my whole lifetime experience involving just one all-too-brief taste, paws up on the kitchen counter, followed by a less-than-pleasant scene with Grammy, not nearly brief enough for me.

"For one thing," Birdie was saying, "it now means both break-ins had the same MO—nothing stolen. That simplifies things, except what's the sheriff going to think when he opens the envelope and sees that photo?"

What was the sheriff going to think? Had I ever heard a tougher question? I didn't even know what I was thinking right now! I checked and found no thoughts present in my mind. Whew.

"He's going to think the laundry hamper story was a total lie," Birdie continued. "Not only that, but someone wanted him to know the truth about the pearls. Who was that someone? That'll be question one."

I waited to find out the identity of that mysterious someone, so curious that the baseball almost slipped from my mouth. I clamped down, got it back under control, nice and tight.

"The sheriff's going to want to talk to the Richelieus. But first he'll want to be prepared. Know what that means, Bowser?"

It sure better not mean taking my baseball. Other than that, I had no ideas.

"His first step," Birdie said, "will be tracking down whoever sent that photo." She gazed down at me. Oh, no! She was worried, easy to see from the tightness of her face, especially between her eyes. "Do you think there's some way of tracing the photo, Bowser? There's a time stamp on it. And maybe he can figure out that it was taken from the Lucinda Street Bridge. And . . . and . . . oh my god! Bowser! There's a surveillance camera on that bridge! Do you see what this means?"

We were going fishing with Junior Tebbets again? That was my best guess.

"It means . . ." Birdie smacked her forehead. I'd never seen her do that before, never wanted to see it again. No one smacked my Birdie, period, and anyone who tried would pay. "It means, Bowser, that we have to get the photo back before the sheriff sees it. Otherwise, he's going to come after us instead of solving the break-in. Not to mention poor Rory."

And then, with no warning, she took off down the street at full speed! Therefore, I took off, too, although not at full speed or anything close. Birdie was fast for a human, but is that really saying much?

We ran down Gentilly Lane, to a blue metal box not far from our house, the same metal box that Birdie had dropped the envelope into the day before. She pulled open the little door and peered inside. "Can't see a thing," she said. "Must be a kind of chute and all the letters fall down to the bottom. Wonder if my arm's long enough to . . ." She stuck her hand in the opening, then noticed some writing on the side of the box. " 'Daily pickup—7:30 a.m.' " She stepped back. "It's gone, Bowser. We're too late." She let go of the little door, which banged shut on its own.

Then we just stood there, the hot sun high in the sky.

"What are we going to do?" Birdie said.

First, find some shade. Second, lap up nice, cool water. And since we're so close to home, practically right across the street—and home had plenty of shade and water—what was wrong with the two of us heading on over there this very minute? I made a little sidling move in that direction, but Birdie didn't seem to get the hint.

"What happens to the mail?" Birdie said. "You put it in this box and then the mailman comes and puts it into your box at home, but what happens in between? They have systems for everything so . . ." She snapped her fingers. What a sound! It sent a little shiver right though me, all the way to my tail and back again. Do it again, Birdie, do it again!

But she did not. "The post office!" she said, and started up on a long, impossible-to-follow explanation about post offices, and mail, and sorting, and maybe even something called the pony express, which didn't sound promising to me, ponies being a kind of horse and therefore unreliable. Meanwhile, we were on the move again, back toward the center of town. We passed Claymore's General Store, got waved at by Mrs. Claymore, out sweeping the porch, and entered a building with a cool stone floor. The place smelled strongly of paper and glue. There was no one inside except the woman behind the counter.

"What can I do for you?" the woman said.

155

"Um," said Birdie. "It's about a letter."

"You need stamps?"

"No. I already mailed the letter. I'd like to stop it. Get it back, kind of, before it gets to . . . to where it was going."

"You want an intercept?"

"I guess so."

"No problem," said the woman. She reached for a sheet of paper on a shelf, slid it across the counter. "Just fill in Form 1509. And I'll need eleven dollars and fifty cents."

"Today?" Birdie said.

"I'm sorry?"

"You'll need the money today?"

"Can't process the form without it."

Birdie gazed at Form 1509. Her eyes went back and forth. "All these questions," she said.

"Answer as best you can."

"What about this one?" Birdie said, pointing out something partway down the page and turning it so the woman could see.

"That's where you put your reason for the intercept."

"My reason?"

"Like you forgot to write the address," the woman said. "Or—"

A mailman, easy to identify from his uniform and the sack of mail over his shoulder—me and my kind get to know mailmen very well—came out from a room behind the counter and said, "Phone's for you."

"You can get started," the woman said to Birdie. "I'll be right back." And she disappeared into the room behind the counter. The mailman opened a little swinging door and came into the lobby. He took a step or two toward the door, then stopped and patted his pockets.

"Forget my head if it wasn't screwed on," he said to Birdie.

Oh, no! The mailman's head was screwed on? That didn't sound like a good arrangement to me, in fact, kind of scary. I hunched down and backed away from him. Meanwhile, he laid his sack of mail on the counter, went through the swinging door and into the back room. His head remained attached the whole time, and I relaxed at least a little bit.

Birdie stared at the sack of mail. She shot a glance at the front door to the post office. Closed, no one coming in. Then she looked my way, like she wanted something from me. Anything, Birdie, anything at all. As for the particulars of what she wanted, I had no idea, but maybe she got it anyway, because she strode right up to that sack of mail in two steps and stuck her hand inside. That was exciting! I trotted over to her and rose up, getting my front paws on the counter. Side by side we rummaged through the mail,

Birdie doing the actual rummaging, her face practically inside the sack. The only sound in the post office was the rippling of envelopes and the beating of Birdie's heart, way too fast, in my opinion. All at once she whipped out a letter, and held it in the light.

"Got it!" she whispered, and slipped the envelope inside her T-shirt. "Let's go!"

We were leaving so soon? No more rummaging or chit-chat with the post office folks? A fun visit so far, except for the problem with the mailman's head, but if Birdie said we were going, we went. And pretty fast, Birdie pretty much running toward the front door and me trotting by her side. She flung the door open and we hurried down the street. Just before the door closed, I heard the faint voice of the post office woman trailing after us.

"What happened to the kid and her dog?"

"Asking me to explain kids?" said the mailman. "Way above my pay grade."

Back in Birdie's room, she took the envelope out from under her T-shirt, removed the photo of Miranda and the pearls, and gave it a look. "Here's a thought, Bowser," she said.

I had plenty of space for it at the moment. Birdie's timing was perfect.

"Mrs. Richelieu saw me with the camera up on the bridge. Is it possible she figured out what I was doing? And

158

then realized that her whole insurance scam idea or whatever it was might be in trouble? Which is how come the pearls ended up getting found in a laundry hamper?"

So complicated! There wasn't a thing I could do to help Birdie with this one.

"No way," she went on. "How could she have figured all that out for sure? But then . . . I just don't know. How else could she have known about the photo?" I had no idea. "But we need to watch out for Mrs. Richelieu—that's for sure."

Oh, that was all? Not a problem. I told myself, *Bowser, watch out for Mrs. Richelieu*. Was barking at her at every sighting a good idea? Had to be. What about biting her, too? I gave that some thought, went back and forth. Biting was a no-no—I knew that. At the same time, I could never allow anything bad to happen to Birdie. And there was no denying that biting Vin Pardo had worked out nicely, unless I was missing something.

Meanwhile, Birdie was tapping the edge of the photo against her teeth, lost in thought. "Know what we need?"

My guess was a snack.

"A hidey-hole," Birdie went on. "A safe little hidey-hole known only to us."

She cast a careful look around our bedroom. Something important was going on—I had no doubt about that. Would we be keeping snacks in the hidey-hole of ours? That was as far as I could take it.

Birdie's gaze finally came to rest on a grate in the ceiling, one of those grates for covering air vents. We had a few in the house, such as the one in Grammy's bedroom, the vent with the fluttering sound inside. This grate in our bedroom was over the bed.

"Aha!" she said. The next thing I knew Birdie had placed her desk chair on the bed—the fun we were about to have!—and started climbing on top of it. Of course, that was where I wanted to be, too. Sometimes in this life, there's just no containing yourself. Maybe most of the time in my case. I hope that's not a problem.

"Bowser!"

Soon after that we were picking ourselves off the floor, no harm done. Our next try was just as much fun or more—Birdie actually balancing on the tippy chair and reaching the rolled-up photo toward a hole in the grate—before the containing-myself period came to an end.

"Once more," Birdie said as we picked ourselves up again, "and I'll have to put you out in the hall and close the door."

Oh, no, not that again! And so soon!

"And cool it with the whimpering!" Birdie said. "We don't whimper in this family."

Whimpering? I thought I heard it, too. I listened my hardest. The whimpering died away. I sat down, if you

160

could still call it sitting when your butt isn't quite touching the floor. Birdie picked up the chair, set it on the bed, climbed up, gave me a quick, anxious glance—about what I had no idea—and slid the rolled-up photo through a hole in the grate and into the vent. She was just climbing down when our door opened.

Grammy took in the scene. "What in heaven's name is going on?"

"Um, we were just sort of . . . playing a game," Birdie said. "Me and Bowser."

"A game, huh?" Grammy gave me a look that could have been friendlier. "I'm starting to think that this mutt's a bad influence on you."

"You don't mean that, Grammy."

"Hrrmf," said Grammy. "And speaking of bad influences, the Tebbets boy is at the front door."

"Junior?" said Birdie. "A bad influence?"

"The Tebbetses have been bad influences in these parts for generations."

"You liked that po'boy, Grammy."

"So? Bad people can be good cooks."

"They can?"

Grammy gave Birdie a long look. Her face softened the littlest bit. "Maybe not often."

thirteen

BROUGHT MY DRUMSTICKS THIS TIME," Junior said as Birdie and I went outside.

"I see that," Birdie said.

"I can play as we go," Junior said.

"What are you talking about?"

At that moment we happened to be passing the blue mailbox on the other side of Gentilly Lane. "Like this," Junior said. He gave the drumsticks a quick twirl and then rat-a-tat-tatted something fast and loud on the mailbox. Birdie closed her eyes tight and Junior stopped right away.

"Got a headache?" he said, drumsticks poised in midair.

Birdie opened her eyes. "No."

"Whew. My stepmom—the new one—does that eyes closing thing when she gets headaches, and she gets headaches all the time."

"I'm fine," Birdie said.

"You didn't like that beat?" said Junior. "Is that it? I've got hundreds more, maybe thousands."

"That's a lot."

"How many do you think Drea will want to hear?"

"Of your beats?" Birdie said. "Why not ask her?"

"Hey! Hadn't thought of that."

I was starting to like Junior more and more. I gave him a friendly bump, very gentle. He didn't even fall down, not all the way.

Mr. Santini stuck out his potbelly and narrowed his eyes, not his best look, in my opinion. "You kids back again?"

"Yup," said Junior.

"Yup? That's how you address your elders?"

"Sorry, elder," Junior said.

Mr. Santini gazed at Junior, a twitch starting up in the side of his face. He turned to Birdie. "Any chance that grandmother of yours would put up a campaign poster at the store next election season?"

"I could ask," said Birdie.

"Fair enough," Mr. Santini said. "Lookin' for the biker gal?"

"We are," Birdie said.

"Workin' on that music reading competition?"

"Gotta get it down cold," said Junior.

Mr. Santini turned back to Junior. "Only way to win. You gonna win?"

"Try my hardest," said Junior.

"Tryin's good," Mr. Santini said. "Winnin's better. So win! Good for the town when our people win."

"It is?" Birdie said.

"Of course—stands to reason." Mr. Santini stepped aside. "Go on down. Haven't seen her yet today." He checked his watch. "Gettin' on four o'clock. Musician's hours."

We walked down the middle path—Paradise Way, unless my memory was playing tricks on me, and I've got the trickiest memory around. The air was full of buzzing insects, their buzzing so loud I could hardly hear myself think, so I gave up the idea of even trying. Did all that buzzing bother Birdie and Junior? Didn't seem to. I wondered whether they even heard it. Human ears? A big puzzle.

"So, uh," Junior said, "you've got a great arm, huh?"

"What do mean?" said Birdie.

"You know. For pitching."

Birdie stopped and turned to him, hands on her hips. "Where'd you hear that?"

Junior shrugged. "Word gets around."

Birdie stood there, hands on hips, and blew air through her lips, making that cool vibration I like. It cut right through the insect drone, maybe even silencing it.

"You mad or something?" Junior said.

"What kind of town is this?" Birdie said. "How come everybody's in everybody else's business?"

"Dunno," Junior said.

Birdie lowered her hands and we walked on, rounding the bend on Paradise Way. The scummy pond came into view, Drea's green tent standing near the shore, with her motorcycle parked out front.

"Baseball's a drag, if you want my opinion," Junior said.

"I don't."

"Not sayin' everyone who thinks baseball's their life is a drag," Junior went on. "Mentioning no names. Rory, for example."

Birdie gave him a look.

"See?" said Junior. "I knew you were mad."

"I'm not mad."

"You look mad."

"I'm not, so don't say it again."

"I'll just think it."

Birdie sped up. I sped up with her. We opened some space between us and Junior, and came to the tent ahead of him. The flap was closed and no sounds came from inside.

"Um, hello," Birdie said. "Drea? It's me, Birdie."

"And Junior," Junior said, coming up beside us. "Brought my sticks today."

Silence. Not even the sound of a human peacefully sleeping, one of my favorite sounds, especially when the sleeper was Birdie.

"Probably napping," Junior said. "Musician's hours." He raised his voice. "Drea! Wakey wakey!"

Nothing but silence from inside the tent. Junior twirled his drumsticks and played a quick *tat-a-tat-tat* on the side of the tent.

"Don't," Birdie said.

"Why not?" said Junior. But he stopped drumming. "How come you're in such a bad mood today?"

Birdie didn't answer. She glanced around Drea's campsite. No sign of Drea, if that was what she was looking for. A tiny breeze wafted by and I caught a very faint scent I didn't like at all. I got my nose up and sniffed, but the scent was gone.

"Maybe she went for a walk," Junior said.

"Yeah," said Birdie. We went for a walk ourselves, checking out the campsites around Drea's. They were all unoccupied except for one, where an old couple sat on lawn chairs, the woman smoking, the man cutting his fingernails.

"Excuse me," Birdie called to them. "Have you seen Drea?"

"Drea?" said the woman.

"From space ninety-six on Paradise Way."

The man looked up. "We're hunnert and forty-two."

"She's not askin' for that," the woman snapped at him. "She's askin' for—what was it again?"

"Drea," Birdie said. She pointed. "Her tent's back that way. She's got kind of greenish hair."

"Don't know nobody with greenish hair," said the woman.

"But I'd kinda like to," said the man quietly.

"What did you just say?" said the woman.

"Nuthin'."

We went back to Drea's tent. Junior gazed out at the pond. "Maybe she's gone for a swim."

"Who'd want to swim in that?" Birdie said.

Me, for one, especially if there was a chance of meeting up with a certain frog of my acquaintance. We moved down to the edge of the pond. The water was still, not a ripple on the surface. No one swimming; no frog soaking up rays on a lily pad. But I did pick up Drea's scent, so maybe she had gone for a swim at some point. What did humans do after a swim? They changed out of their bathing suits and back into regular clothes. Me and my kind just gave ourselves a good shake, so much simpler.

We returned to the tent. Did Birdie think Drea might be changing inside? Even though no breathing was happening in there? Although it's true that sometimes humans held their breath. Once Nola and Birdie had a contest about who could hold their breath the longest. I never wanted to see that again.

Birdie raised a corner of the flap and peeked inside.

"See anything?" Junior said.

"Looks . . . normal. Maybe she drove out in a car with another camper or something."

"Yeah, shoulda thought of that. We gonna wait?"

"Can't hurt to wait a little—whoa." Birdie squinted into the tent.

"Whoa?"

Birdie raised the flap some more and moved inside.

"Okay to do this?" Junior said. "Kind of like somebody's house, isn't it?"

Birdie didn't answer. By that time I was in the tent myself. Everything looked normal, as Birdie had said. There was an open motorcycle saddlebag on the floor, a pair of blue jeans neatly folded on top. Also, an unrolled sleeping bag, zipped up, lying on an inflatable pad. But— what was this? In the shadows between the sleeping bag and the side of the tent, lay Drea's guitar, totally wrecked.

Birdie went over and picked it up. A string caught on something and made a jangly twang, horrible to my ears.

"What happened to her guitar?" Junior said.

168

Birdie held it up. The neck was just about snapped in two and the body was twisted and broken. Junior said, "Who was that rock star, used to smash his guitar at every performance?"

"I don't know," Birdie said. "But how could this be that?"

Junior nodded. He came forward and took the guitar in a gentle way and then just sort of held it. Meanwhile, Birdie looked around some more and sniffed the air.

"Smells swampy in here," she said.

Birdie was right about that. So nice to find out that little nose of hers could at least do something. But who could have missed the swampy smell in Drea's tent, so strong I smelled nothing else?

"This is one of those real spongy parts of town," Junior said.

"Spongy?"

"The ground. Like the swamp is sneaking up underneath."

"That sounds like a bad dream."

"Got the idea from a bad dream, actually," Junior said.

"You have lots of them?" said Birdie.

"Bad dreams? Wouldn't say lots. Maybe once every— hey. What's this?" He turned the guitar over, revealing a yellowed and worn strip of paper glued to the inside of what remained of the body. Birdie leaned in.

"Looks like a newspaper clipping," she said. "Just the banner at the top. The rest is torn away."

"New Orleans *Times-Picayune*," Junior said. "Page three from September fourth, two thousand and—something or other. Last two numbers are gone." He looked up. "How come she keeps this inside her guitar? Probably on account of whatever's in the missing part, huh?"

"Unless it's the date itself," said Birdie.

"A birthday or something like that?" Junior said.

"No clue," Birdie said. "We'll just have to ask her."

"Maybe there's something written on the back." Junior pinched a corner of the old newspaper strip between his finger and thumb and peeled it off the wood. Or tried to. What happened was that the whole newspaper strip just sort of crumbled to dust.

"Uh-oh," Junior said. He quickly laid the broken guitar on the sleeping bag and stepped away. "Think she's upset about something?"

"Like what?"

"Like she was trying to play some song and couldn't get it right?"

"So she smashed up her guitar?" Birdie said.

"Yeah," Junior said. His forehead wrinkled up. "Who was that painter who cut off his ear?"

"Van somebody," said Birdie. "Did he do that because he was having trouble with a painting?"

"Why else would he?"

" 'Cause maybe he was crazy," Birdie said.

Junior thought about that. "You think Drea's crazy?"

Birdie shook her head.

"She has that green hair," said Junior.

"You have a Mohawk."

"And I'm crazy as a loon."

Birdie laughed.

"Least that's what my dad says," Junior added.

Birdie stopped laughing.

We left the tent, stood outside. Junior paced around a bit, drumsticks loose in his hand, kind of like he'd forgotten about them. Birdie walked over to the motorcycle, touched the tailpipe with her toe. I followed Drea's scent down to the water.

"What should we do?" Birdie said.

"About what?" said Junior.

"About . . . about Drea saying to come at four and now we're here and . . ."

"How about we wait for a few more minutes?" Junior said.

"Okay."

We waited. After a very short time, I barked.

"Bowser, what are you barking about?"

I barked again.

"Cool it."

I pawed at the edge of the water and barked some more, a high-pitched bark that irritates everybody, me included.

"What's buggin' him?" Junior said.

"He seems to get funny around this pond," said Birdie. "Come here, Bowser."

Junior gazed at the pond. "It is kind of nasty. Are a few minutes up yet?"

Birdie toed the tailpipe again. "I guess so. Bowser! Come!"

Junior was right about the nastiness of the pond. I didn't want to hang around it any longer. But wasn't it part of my job? To stay there until somebody did something?

"Bowser!"

I stood by the edge of the pond, mouth open, possibly panting slightly.

"Bowser? Are you all right?" Birdie hurried over, knelt, and took my face in her hands. She looked worried. About me? The last thing I wanted. I gave myself a good shake, shaking off whatever had been bothering me, and the three of us walked back up Paradise Way.

Mr. Santini was by the gate, wearing earphones and whacking weeds with a weed whacker. He shut it down as we approached, raising the earphones off one ear.

"How'd it go, Junior?" he said. "Gonna kill 'em?"

172

"Kill?" said Junior. "Kill who?"

"Whoever. In the music competition."

"Uh, I didn't have a lesson."

"Drea wasn't there," Birdie said. "She must have gone out."

"Out? Out like offa the campground?"

"Yeah," Birdie said.

Mr. Santini shook his head. "I been right here the whole day. Breakin' my back in the hot sun. I'da seen her if she'd of gone out."

"Maybe she went by the back way," Birdie said.

"Ain't no back way. Swamp closes in on both sides, more muck than water. Anybody goes in or out, they do it right here."

"Oh," Birdie said.

"Oh," said Junior.

We all stood around. Finally, Mr. Santini said, "So she's gotta be on the property, is what I'm sayin'."

"Okay," Birdie said. "We'll look around."

"Best part of six acres," said Mr. Santini. "Be faster in a golf cart."

Which was how I ended up riding in a golf cart for the very first time! What a great human invention! Mr. Santini, who didn't like kids and dogs, was turning out to be not too bad. He drove, Junior up front beside him, Birdie and

173

me in back. I sat nice and tall, the breeze rippling through my coat in the most refreshing way.

"We'll start down Heavenly Road," Mr. Santini said, "then take the short cut to Glory."

Birdie laughed.

"What's funny?" Junior said.

"Search me," said Mr. Santini.

We rode up and down the lanes of the campground. Sometimes we spotted campers and stopped for a little chat. We got lots of shoulder shrugs and blank looks. After a while we were back at the gate, ride over. Too soon, in my opinion. Couldn't we go around again? But no.

Mr. Santini switched off the engine, rubbed his chin. "Hmm," he said. "Musta gotten out somehow." A big bird squawked and shot up in the sky from a nearby tree. "She'll turn up," said Mr. Santini.

fourteen

EXT MORNING, BIRDIE WAS VERY SLEEPY. Just before daylight, I heard Mama get up. Then came shower sounds, and not long after that, footsteps right up to our door.

"Birdie?" Mama called in a low voice.

I glanced over at Birdie. Although I started most nights on my small, round doggy bed on the floor, I usually ended up on her bed—well, our bed, really, mine and Birdie's. For some reason she seemed to be squished up against the wall on this particular morning. Her eyes were closed, her breathing soft. Mama moved back down the hall. Not long after that, I heard Mama and Grammy talking out on the breezeway. A few moments later, two car doors opened and closed. The car drove off: Mama's car, with Grammy in the shotgun seat, if I was reading things right. Don't count on it. I wriggled in closer to Birdie.

"Bowser," she said in a kind of groan. "A little space."

A little space? What did that mean, again? We needed to get closer together? Was it even possible, what with how close we were already? But I'm not the type who gives up easily, especially when it comes to doing what Birdie wants. Therefore, I gave it my very best shot, digging my paws into the covers, getting my best grip, and squeezing in like I meant it. Which I did! So I squeezed and squeezed and—

"Bowser!"

Then came what you might call a crash, although not a loud one, and Birdie was no longer in the bed. Instead, she seemed to have fallen off, down into the very narrow space between the bed and the wall. Was this a brand-new game? Who was more fun than Birdie? Was my next move to crawl down with her in the very narrow space?

"BOWSER!"

Perhaps not.

Soon after that, we were in the kitchen, chowing down— Birdie on cereal with banana slices and me on good old kibble, my go-to meal, although I can't think of any food I don't like. I cleaned my bowl in no time flat, but what was this? Birdie just picking at her food? Was something bothering her?

She looked my way. "Do you think she came back?"

I had no thoughts on that, didn't even have a clue who Birdie was talking about.

"Maybe I should call the campground."

Something about the campground? I thought of the scummy, buggy pond and decided I wasn't really in the mood for a campground visit today. How about swinging by the store and hanging out with Grammy and Snoozy instead?

Meanwhile, Birdie was punching the buttons on the kitchen phone. She listened and hung up.

"Answering machine," she said. She drummed her fingers on the counter. I loved the sound of that! Humans were just about at their very best when they were drumming their fingers, in my opinion. More, more, more! But there was no more. Birdie turned to me and said, "Let's head over there." And moments later, we were out the door, heading to wherever "over there" might be.

It was light outside now, the air at its freshest. I felt my very best. Along the way I marked a tree or two—plus a rosebush and a fire hydrant, and possibly the wheel of a bicycle chained to a telephone pole—and felt even better. We were approaching the library—a white wooden building with pale blue trim and a pale blue roof—when a solidly built man with shoulder-length hair and a stack of books in his arms hurried past us. He was a few steps ahead when he stopped and glanced back.

"Birdie?" he said.

"Hi, Mr. Savoy."

Mr. Savoy ran the library, if I remembered right, also played the accordion.

"And," he went on, "the famous Bowser."

A great guy, Mr. Savoy. I almost left that out.

"Looks like he's grown some," said Mr. Savoy. "Must be eating you out of house and home."

Not that again! What did it even mean?

"Well," Birdie said, "um."

Exactly my own thoughts!

Mr. Savoy laughed. Then his eyes shifted and he said, "I hear your mom's back."

"Yeah."

"That must be nice."

Birdie nodded.

"I expect she's exhausted after those assignments."

"She's okay," Birdie said.

"Good to hear," said Mr. Savoy. "Uh, please give her my best." He turned to the brick walk that led to the library door. "Time to open up. Any book you'd like to borrow while you're here?"

"No, thanks," Birdie said. "We're on our way to—" She paused. "Mr. Savoy?"

"Yes?"

"Do you—I mean does the library—collect old newspapers?"

"Collect? As in paper form? Mostly we're digital these days, but we've got stacks of old papers up in the loft."

"Oh."

"Any particular old newspapers you're interested in?"

"The New Orleans *Times-Picayune*."

"No problem. We've got every edition going back for at least a century, maybe longer. Any special date you're looking for?"

"September fourth," Birdie said.

"What year?"

"Two thousand and something."

Mr. Savoy gazed down at Birdie. He had a strong sort of face, but it seemed gentle, a combination I wasn't used to on the men in these parts. "That narrows it down some," he said.

"The rest was torn off," Birdie said. "It was mostly all torn off."

"Ah," said Mr. Savoy. "Let's see what we can do."

The library smelled like no other place I knew, so papery. And nothing smells more papery than old newspapers. Mr. Savoy had gotten Birdie settled at a scuffed-up table in the library loft, laid a stack of old newspapers in front of her. "Here's the entire twenty-first century, so far," he'd said, and gone away. Although not far. From where I lay—in a pool of golden sunlight at Birdie's feet—I could sort of feel him standing at the bottom of the stairs that led to the loft.

Up above me, Birdie turned the pages. A very enjoyable sound, crisp and fluttery at the same time. I gazed at her feet. She wore blue flip-flops with silver stars on the straps. Her feet were very still, and seemed to be concentrating on something, like they had minds of their own. Which they probably did: My tail was the same way. Because of how preoccupied Birdie's feet seemed to be I held off on licking them, which had been my first thought.

From time to time she muttered things, like "page three, page three." And "nope, nope, nope." After that would come the sound of a newspaper getting lifted off the stack and plunked in a new pile, and then more of the crispy flutters. So nice of Birdie to entertain me like this! I gave the nearest foot a lick after all. It . . . it shifted away, like it had something else going on. That was bothersome. I tried to think of what to do next, and hadn't come up with anything, before Birdie went tense and sat up very straight, her toes curling. Her toenails, by the way, were painted blue, which maybe I should have mentioned before.

"Oh, Bowser. This is so . . . so . . . oh, no!" She leaned forward, the side of her face coming into my field of view. I could see only one of those eyes of hers, normally summer-sky blue but now much more like the color of clouds. That eye went back and forth real fast, and when Birdie spoke again her voice was low, tense, even afraid.

" 'Local Man Murdered. New Orleans police are investigating the murder of Henry R. Bolden, a real estate developer in the city. His bullet-riddled body was discovered last night floating near the west bank of Bayou St. John, close to the foot of Friedrichs Avenue. Detective Captain Robert Gaux is in charge of the case. Reached by telephone, he said that the police are pursuing several leads and had no further comment.' "

Birdie put her hands on the table and slowly pushed herself up, like her legs had lost their strength. She looked down at me, her eyes open wide, although I got the strange feeling she wasn't really seeing me. Poor Birdie! Her face was so pale. Why? I had no idea. I rose and pressed up against her, all I could think of to do. Her hand moved, found the back of my neck, rested on it.

"Henry R. Bolden," Birdie said, starting to talk faster and faster. "Bolden, Bowser! Didn't Drea say her last name was Bolden? So he had to be her dad. What about my own dad? Did she know he was dead, too? She must have! Then why did she pretend she was hearing it for the first time when I told her? What's she up to?"

I pressed against her a little harder, pitching in as best I could.

"And that's not all! There's so much more I can barely think. That September was when my dad got killed. So was this the case he was working on at the end? The case that never got solved? What is going on?" She gave her head a quick shake, ridding her eyes of that distant stare. "Come on, Bowser. We need to talk to Drea."

We ran down the stairs from the loft. Mr. Savoy was standing at a coffee machine not far away, his back to us. He turned slowly, the coffee cup held kind of casually but his eyes very watchful.

"Birdie? Find what you were looking for?"

"Uh, thanks, Mr. Savoy. Yeah, I think so."

We headed for the front door.

"Anything I can help you with?"

"No, thanks, Mr. Savoy." Birdie opened the door.

"You know where to find me," Mr. Savoy called after us.

I glanced back, caught sight of him starting up the stairs to the loft. Had Birdie folded up the newspaper she'd been reading, or left it open on the table? I couldn't remember. And why was I even having a thought like that?

"Negative," said Mr. Santini, back at the campground gate. No weed whacking today. Instead, he was on his knees, slapping white paint on the rocks that lined the roadside. "She never came back last night. I swung by first thing this morning in the cart. She's not there. Most likely staying with someone in town." He pointed the paintbrush

182

at us. "Campsite charges accrue daily, irregardless of occupancy."

"Can we go down there anyway?" Birdie said.

Mr. Santini shrugged. "Don't see why not. Or why, for that matter."

"So we can or we can't?"

"Can," said Mr. Santini. At that moment he noticed that paint was dripping off the brush and onto his pants. The sight made him say something I'm sure he didn't mean.

Birdie and I walked down Paradise Way to the green tent by the pond.

"Drea?" Birdie called. But only once. Then she drew back the tent flap and checked inside. No Drea, and everything looked exactly as it had the day before. "Mr. Santini must be right—she's staying with someone in town." We went over to the motorcycle. Birdie poked at the tailpipe with her foot. "But how come she didn't take her ride? I guess there could be reasons. Except why have to depend on someone else? When you've got your own motorcycle? See what I mean, Bowser?"

I did not. Meanwhile, we were wandering down to the edge of the pond. Scummy, murky, buggy: Nothing had changed. Somehow even the lily pads looked ugly. Tiny insects scurried here and there across the still surface of the water, like they were up to something. I did not like this pond. I gazed across to the trees on the other side. Was that where I'd first spotted Vin Pardo, lurking around with his binoculars? Or had I seen him before that, driving slowly past 19 Gentilly Lane in his sporty two-seater, cat on the back shelf? And was the cat named Bonnie? How hard it was to keep all this straight in your mind! I knew from experience that I wasn't going to be able to do it for much longer. Birdie! A little help, here!

She was gazing out at the pond. "I love the water, Bowser," she said. "And I love the swamp. But something about this pond . . ."

I waited for her to go on, but instead she just went back to gazing. All of a sudden an enormous bubble rose up from the depths of the pond, not far from us, and burst on the surface. The pop it made sounded very loud to my ears.

Birdie's eyes narrowed. "Could be something with the water table," she said. "Or . . . or something rotting down there." She stepped forward, actually putting one foot in the water. A soft breeze was blowing toward us across the pond, and at that moment it brought me the smells that had been in that bubble. The next thing I knew, I was standing in the pond myself, up to my chest and barking my head off.

"Bowser! What is it?"

I barked and barked and didn't stop.

■ ■ ■

We ran up to the gate. Mr. Santini was taking a break, leaning against the gatehouse and drinking a soda.

"Mr. Santini! Mr. Santini! Do you have a mask and snorkel?"

"Huh? What for would I be wanting any of that? I don't know how to swim."

"You don't?"

"And I'm proud of it!"

"But—but we have to see down into the pond!"

"What for?"

"Because . . . because I think she . . . she . . ."

Mr. Santini gave Birdie a long look. Then he pushed away from the gatehouse and set his soda aside. "I got a glass-bottom bucket," he said. "And there's a rowboat down at the end of Heavenly Road."

Not long after that we were in the rowboat. I love boats, myself, usually ride up front in what they call the bow. But Birdie was in the bow this time, in charge of the glass-bottom bucket. Mr. Santini was on the bench, facing forward and in charge of the rowing. I stood between them, in charge of everything else.

"A little more that way, Mr. Santini," Birdie said, and we changed direction a bit. She lifted her hand, made a pushing motion against the air. Mr. Santini raised the oar blades out of the water and we slowed down. Birdie knelt, leaned over the side, lowered the bucket into the water, and peered down through the glass bottom. From where I was, now sort of right beside her, I caught a quick glimpse myself. Hey! You could see through the water pretty clearly through that bucket. I even spotted a fat brown fish swimming by, before Birdie kind of squeezed me out. Not on purpose, of course.

We glided along real slow, nothing to hear but the water rippling against the hull. Birdie, her back to Mr. Santini, pointed out toward the open water. Mr. Santini took one of the oars out of its lock and used it as a paddle, changing our direction. Birdie gave him the pushing motion again, and we slowed back down, barely drifting along. She leaned out farther and farther, so her head was almost in the bucket and most of her was outside the boat. A bad idea, in my opinion. I was considering getting a grip on her T-shirt and pulling her back in a bit when her whole body went stiff.

"STOP!"

fifteen

SHERIFF CANNON AND OFFICER PERKINS
drove up in a big pickup towing a trailer with a
police launch on the back. They put yellow tape
all around Drea's campsite and then got busy with the
launch. The trailer bogged down at the side of the pond
almost right away. Mr. Santini made a suggestion or two.
The sheriff snapped at him. Mr. Santini snapped right
back. Campers from Heavenly Road, Paradise Way, and
Glory Street gathered around behind the yellow tape. The
sheriff yelled at them to go on home. They backed up a
step or two. The sheriff told Mr. Santini to get all those
people the heck out of there. Mr. Santini told the people to
get the heck out of there. They backed up another step
or two. As for me and Birdie, we watched from the little
dock at the end of Glory Street, where Mr. Santini had tied
up the rowboat. No one paid any attention to us, off by
ourselves.

After what seemed like a long time, the launch was
motoring slowly across the pond, the sheriff at the wheel,
Perkins on a seat in the middle, Mr. Santini in the bow,

pointing this way and that. Birdie just watched, not saying a word. Like her, I watched what was happening on the pond, but I also kept an eye on Birdie, which was my job, after all. She seemed to be trembling a bit, even though it wasn't the slightest bit cold. In fact, it was the hottest time of day. The khaki uniform shirts of the sheriff and Perkins were soaked through. Mr. Santini—in a singlet not quite roomy enough to cover his potbelly—looked a little cooler. He raised his hand in the stop sign.

"Right alongside that there lily pad," he said.

The sheriff pulled back the throttle—I've been out on the water with Birdie and Grammy many times, knew all the lingo—and swung the boat around in a tight circle. Perkins bent down and fumbled with something on the deck that I couldn't see. Then he rose up with a device that was new to me. New to me, yes, but there was no mistaking the big hooks at the end of it. Birdie covered her mouth.

I leaned in against her. She put her hand on my back, held on tight. I got the idea that maybe I should steer her away from this pond and herd her back home. I gave her a bit of a push, just to kind of test the idea. Funny enough, I couldn't budge her, and I'm a lot stronger than Birdie. I'm actually stronger than a lot of grown-up humans, too! It's fun being me, although not there on the shore of the pond, where no one was having any fun at all.

The hook device was on the end of a thick chain. Perkins lowered it into the pond, making a small splash that seemed quite loud for some reason. He let the links of the chain run out through his hands.

"Should do it," said Mr. Santini. "Depth maxes out at thirty feet."

Perkins fixed one of the links to a cleat near the bow, stopping the hooks from sinking any lower in the pond. The sheriff turned the wheel and the launch chugged around and around at a very slow speed. No one—not the men on the boat, the campers on the shore, or Birdie— spoke a word. Even the insects had gone silent. I could hear Birdie's heart going *pat-pat*, *pat-pat*. And then there was my own heart, boom-booming away. As for what was happening out on the pond, I had no clue.

The launch—all black, which maybe I should have mentioned before—glided in circles a little while longer, and then seemed to lurch very slightly.

"Whoa!" Perkins said, his deep, rumbly voice shaking the air, at least to my way of hearing.

The sheriff backed the launch up a tiny bit, the engine throbbing low and sending ripples across the water. Perkins began hauling on the chain, grunting once or twice with the effort even though he was such a big guy. The chain rose up from the pond, one dripping link after another.

Then came some weeds, blackish green and mucky, and after that a sight that made all the humans gasp, except for the men on the boat. Some even turned away, although not Birdie. I myself sat down and waited for the smell of death to arrive. It came soon enough.

An ambulance drove slowly down Paradise Way from the direction of the gate. Sheriff Cannon, now back on shore, yelled at people to go home. Mr. Santini said something to him that I couldn't make out. The sheriff snapped at him. Mr. Santini snapped back.

"Come on, Bowser," Birdie said.

We went up Glory Street, left the campground, and walked home. Birdie trembled the whole way. I hated seeing that. And how afraid she was! I could smell just about nothing else except her fear. My tail kept wanting to droop. Up, tail! Up and stay up! It pretty much obeyed me the rest of the way. From time to time I gave Birdie a little nudge, just to remind her that she had me.

No one was home, not in our part of the house or in Grammy's.

"Why, Bowser? Why couldn't somebody just be here?"

Whatever that was, it didn't sound like Birdie to me.

"And what are you barking about?"

Barking? News to me, but I heard barking, beyond any

doubt, and it wasn't coming from Birdie. She reached out and stroked my head.

"You're upset, too, huh?" She kept stroking me, and her trembling settled down to just about nothing. I put a lid on any barking that had been going on and gazed into her eyes: still the color of the sky, yes, but on a cloudy—maybe even stormy—day. We kind of huddled together for a bit.

Birdie rose. "Come on, Bowser."

We opened the door to Gaux Family Fish and Bait—Birdie doing the actual work with the doorknob, me in more of a supporting role—and went inside. Snoozy was alone in the store. He had a rod in his hand and appeared to be practicing his sideways casts. At the moment, he'd hooked a pair of yellow rain pants that was hanging on a clothes rack display.

"Where is everybody?" Birdie said.

"I'm somebody," said Snoozy, reeling in the rain pants.

"I meant Grammy," Birdie said. "Or my mom."

Snoozy unhooked the rain pants. I heard a faint ripping sound.

"Your mom's gone out in the pirogue with that businessman, showing him around."

"What businessman?"

"Nice friendly guy from New Orleans." Snoozy rubbed his finger and thumb together, a human sign you see from time to time, its meaning unknown to me. "Mover-and-shaker type."

"Vin Pardo?"

"Sounds right," Snoozy said. "As for your grammy, she had to go pick up a—"

The door opened behind us and in came Grammy. Her washed-out eyes took in the scene, fastened on Snoozy.

"How many times have I told you?" she said.

"It's not what it looks like," Snoozy said, sort of trying to hide the rod behind his back. "I wasn't really casting in the store. More like showing Birdie here how to—"

Birdie burst into tears and ran to Grammy, throwing her arms around her. Grammy's eyes and mouth opened wide, like she was totally astonished.

"Snoozy!" she said. "What on earth is going on?"

"Me?" said Snoozy. "Me?"

"Oh, Grammy," Birdie cried. "It's so horrible."

"What is, child?" Grammy rubbed Birdie's back. "What happened? Tell me."

I sat down right next to Birdie. That was my place. And what was this? On the other side of Birdie, who should appear but Snoozy, a glass of water in his hand.

"Birdie?" he said quietly. "Water."

Birdie took the glass, sipped from it. She stepped away from Grammy, wiped her eyes with the back of her hand.

"Out with it," Grammy said. "Can't be as bad as all that."

"But it is," Birdie told her. And she started in on a long story, all about Drea, and Junior, and a newspaper clipping in a smashed guitar, and a body at the bottom of Mr. Santini's pond.

Grammy held up her hand. "Bolden?"

"Yes, Grammy."

"But that was the name of the victim on the last case!"

"I know, Grammy. That's why—"

Grammy put her bony hand to her chest. Her face lost all its color, went so white her teeth looked dark yellow. All the strength inside her seemed to leak out at once, and she slumped to the floor.

But not quite. Somehow Snoozy—moving fast not just for him but for any human—leaped forward and caught Grammy in midair. Then, pretty much carrying her bodily, he got her seated in a chair. Birdie still had her water glass. She held it out for Grammy. Grammy took it, her hand so shaky that Birdie had to help her drink. Their heads touched. Grammy's color started coming back.

"You all right, boss?" Snoozy said.

"Of course I'm all right," said Grammy, but in a wheezy little voice. She gave her head an angry little shake that reminded me a lot of Birdie, and tried again. "Of course I'm all right." Now she was back to sounding more like Grammy.

"Just checking," Snoozy said.

Not long after that, we went home. Birdie got Grammy seated at the kitchen table, poured her some ice tea. "Ah," said Grammy. "There's life in tea."

Birdie topped up Grammy's glass to the brim. Grammy picked up the phone, called Mama, got no answer. "Still up the bayou, out of range," she said, taking another sip. Birdie poured herself some limeade. I went over to my bowl and lapped up some water. I wasn't really thirsty—more just being polite—but oddly enough I did turn out to be thirsty after all. Funny how that works! I ended up licking the bowl dry. And then felt kind of proud of myself. Things were going well. Then I remembered that they weren't.

"I just don't understand," Grammy said. "How did you meet this . . . this Drea in the first place?"

"It was on the bridge, Grammy. We were fishing and . . ."

"Who's we?"

"Me and Junior, and—"

There was a knock at the door. A knock at the door and I hadn't even heard footsteps? That was bad. I hurried over there, and through the door I smelled a gun. True, it hadn't been fired recently, but I wasn't taking chances, not on a day like this. I planted myself right in front of the door, made myself very big, and growled my deepest growl.

"Who's there?" Grammy called.

"Sheriff Cannon, ma'am. May I come in?"

Grammy gazed across the table at Birdie. Poor Birdie, looking pale and especially small at the moment. Maybe she didn't know how to make herself big. Although it's possible you need a coat of fur to do that, meaning ol' Bowser hits the jackpot again.

"What's it about?" Grammy said, her voice still raised.

"I'd like to make sure that Birdie's all right."

Grammy lowered her voice. "Okay with you, child?"

Birdie nodded.

"It's open," Grammy called.

The sheriff came in. He took off his hat. "Afternoon, ma'am, Birdie. I'm a little surprised your door's unlocked, Mrs. Gaux, what with the recent break-in and all."

"It's broad daylight, for heaven's sake," Grammy said. "And we're here and wide awake, two people and a dog. What kind of town would it be if we had to lock our doors twenty-four seven?"

"A town like many others," the sheriff said. "Maybe most."

"I surely hope not," said Grammy. She glared at the sheriff.

"I'm with you," he said. "Mind if I sit?"

Grammy gestured toward an empty chair. "Tea?"

"Tea would be real nice," the sheriff said. He sat down, set his hat on his knee, rubbed his chin. I heard a rasping sound, like maybe he hadn't shaved yet today.

Birdie put a glass of tea in front of him, slid over the sugar bowl. He spooned some sugar in his glass, sipped, and took a deep breath.

"Well?" said Grammy.

The sheriff nodded and sat straighter in his chair. He had a big strong face with big strong features, but right now it mostly looked tired. "As you may know already, we fished—excuse me, we recovered the body of Drea Bolden from the pond down at Santini's Campground. Birdie here, I'm sorry to say, was the person who actually discovered the body."

"Sorry to say?" said Grammy. "Why is that?"

"On account of her being a child, of course," the sheriff said.

"She's eleven," Grammy said. "Not a baby."

The sheriff gave Grammy the sort of sideways look one human gives another when human one doesn't quite get where human two is coming from. "You all right, Birdie?" he said.

"Yes, sir," said Birdie, although she now looked even paler to me. "And it was really Bowser who . . . who figured it out."

That Birdie! You had to love her, and I did.

The sheriff smiled a little smile and turned to me. "What else have you figured out, Bowser? I could sure use some help."

What else had I figured out? Wow! What a question! I didn't even know where to begin. That made it pretty easy to forget the whole thing, which I did.

The sheriff took another sip of tea. "Three main points, ma'am, if you'll bear with me. First, cause of death. That's in the hands of the medical examiner, and we won't know until next week, what with how backed up they are and all the budget cuts. But I observed no evidence of anything untoward."

"I don't understand," Birdie said.

"Meaning there was nothing to suggest any cause of death other than accidental drowning."

"But—but what about her guitar?" Birdie said. "It was all smashed up."

"It's my understanding that was all about some sort of artistic frustration," the sheriff said.

"What?" said Birdie. "Who told you that?"

"I caught up with young Junior Tebbets on my way over here. I believe that was what he was telling me."

"He was?" Birdie said.

"Or at least trying to," said the sheriff. "Do you have

any reason to suspect another cause, when it comes to the guitar?"

"There was a sort of newspaper clipping inside," Birdie said.

"Junior mentioned that. We'll be conducting a careful examination of the guitar first thing tomorrow morning."

"But mostly it was gone. Ripped out."

"Junior told me something about that, too, and we'll be looking into it," the sheriff said. "Moving on to point—"

"Back up a bit," Grammy said. "Who'd go swimming in that foul pond in the first place?"

"A surprising number of the campers down there, according to Santini," the sheriff said. "Mr. Santini, that is."

"He'll be watching your investigation closely, is my guess," Grammy said.

"Oh, no doubt," the sheriff said.

"Election coming up," Grammy said.

"True," said the sheriff. "But that won't affect how I do my job, not one bit."

Grammy nodded. "Point two," she said.

"Point two," said the sheriff, "is kind of strange. It appears that Drea Bolden was the daughter of Henry R. Bolden, a real estate developer from New Orleans and the murder victim in the case your son, Captain Gaux, was working on when he . . ." He glanced at Birdie. "When he passed."

Grammy reached for her tea, her hand shaky again. But she got it under control and took a long swig. "Birdie was just informing me of that fact," Grammy said. "If it is a fact."

"Pretty much a certainty," the sheriff said. "I've got a call into—"

At that moment, I heard laughter from out on the breezeway. Mama's laughter, to be precise. We all heard it—Birdie, Grammy, the sheriff, and me—and we all turned toward the door. It opened and there was Mama, looking pretty happy, her face reddened by a day in the sun, a bunch of wildflowers in her hand. Beside her stood Vin Pardo, also looking pretty happy, his face reddened by the sun, as well. In his hand was a bottle of wine with a ribbon tied tight around the neck. One other thing I noticed was a bandage on his forehead, over one eye. It wasn't the smallest bandage I'd ever seen, although you couldn't have called it huge. My fur rose like iron spikes again, from my neck all the way to the tip of my tail. I wished I'd been responsible for whatever had happened to his forehead.

sixteen

MAMA'S HAPPY LOOK WAVERED AND for a moment seemed to hang in the air, like it was separate from her, a very weird sight I didn't need to see again anytime soon. "Uh, hi, everybody. Hello, Sheriff."

The sheriff nodded. "Mrs. Gaux," he said.

Mama glanced at Birdie, then at Grammy. "Is . . . is everything all right?"

"No," said the sheriff. "I can't say that everything is all right. Far from it. I'm afraid there's been a drowning down at Santini's pond. Birdie discovered the body."

"Oh, no," Mama said. She left Pardo's side, hurried over to Birdie, bent forward kind of awkwardly—down to Birdie's sitting level—put her hands on Birdie's arms, and gazed at her face. "Are you okay, sweetheart? Are you okay?"

Birdie gave her a brisk nod for yes, although her eyes filled with tears at the same time. Mama held her tight and didn't let go. At the same time, she looked across the table at the sheriff. "Who . . . who drowned? Was it someone we know?"

"As for that," the sheriff began, and then stopped and turned toward Pardo, still standing in the doorway.

Pardo raised his hands in one of those human who-me gestures. "Sorry to have stumbled in at a bad time," he said. "Thanks for the tour, Jen. I'll be getting along."

"And you are?" said the sheriff.

"This is Vin Pardo," Mama said. "Vin, Sheriff Cannon."

"Pleased to meet you, Sheriff," Pardo said. "I . . . hope it's nothing too serious."

"A drowning is always serious," said the sheriff.

"Of course," said Pardo. "Stupid of me to put it like that. What I meant was I hoped Jen and her family won't be too troubled." He came into the room a step or two, set the bottle of wine on the counter. "Let me know if there's anything I can do, Jen," he said and turned for the door.

"Where you from, Mr. Pardo?" the sheriff said.

"New Orleans," said Pardo, stopping but not turning to look back. Was he waiting for the sheriff to say something more. Maybe about the wine? That was my only guess.

"Have a nice day," the sheriff said, which I hadn't thought of at all. Pardo went out and closed the door.

Mama pulled up a chair and sat close to Birdie. There were little rosy splotches on her cheeks, like she was blushing a bit, blushing something you see from time to time on female faces, not so often with boys and never with men, and about which I understand zip.

"How . . . how did this happen?" she said.

"As I was saying when you arrived," the sheriff told her, "we're waiting on the medical examiner's report. But neither I nor Officer Perkins nor the EMTs observed anything to indicate causes other than accidental drowning. That being said—"

"How can you tell accidental drowning from drowning on purpose?" Grammy broke in, her voice, always pretty sharp, now at its sharpest.

The sheriff sat up straight. "That usually involves other forms of evidence. A note left behind or"—he shot a quick glance at Birdie—"a letter sent to a friend, for example. What I meant was we found no signs of violence."

"But . . . but the guitar," Birdie said.

The sheriff sighed. "Birdie's referring to a broken guitar that the—"

Mama interrupted the sheriff, waved her hand like she was shooing away flies. We had no flies in the kitchen at the moment and hardly ever did, on account of Grammy being so strict about keeping the screens closed. She was also deadly with the swatter, should a fly or two happen to sneak in.

"Slow down. Please. What I meant was how did it

happen that my daughter was the one who discovered the . . . who discovered all this? I don't understand."

"Actually," the sheriff said, "that's something I'm not too clear about myself. I was wondering if Birdie could fill in some of the blanks."

Everyone turned to Birdie. Everyone except me. I kept a close watch on the sheriff.

"Fill in the blanks?" she said. "Like how?"

"Well," said the sheriff, "how did you meet Drea Bolden in the first place?" He turned to Mama. "That being the name of the deceased."

"Bolden?" Mama said. She put her hand to her chest, just as Grammy had done back at the store. I had the craziest thought of my life: Where's Snoozy? But we didn't end up needing him. Mama held on to her strength. "Bolden?" she said. "That was the name of—"

The sheriff held up his hand. "We'll get to that."

"Oh my god," Mama said, shrinking back in her chair.

"Please continue, Birdie," said the sheriff.

"It was on the bridge," Birdie said. "We were fishing, me and Junior, and she—Drea—drove up on her motorcycle."

"And that was the first time you met her?" the sheriff said.

"Yes."

"Ever in your whole life? You're sure about that?"

Birdie nodded.

"What's up?" Grammy said. "You're saying Birdie knew her from before?"

"No, ma'am," said the sheriff. "Just making certain I've got things straight in my own mind. But," he continued, his eyes now on Birdie, "since your grandmother put it that way, namely knowing rather than meeting, is it possible you knew Drea from before?"

"From before?" Birdie said.

"From before she drove up on her motorcycle," said the sheriff.

"She was from New Orleans," Grammy said. "How could the child possibly have known her from before?"

"Supposing Drea had gotten in touch at some point in the past," the sheriff said. "By sending Birdie a letter, for example."

"Did that ever happen, sweetheart?" Mama said.

"No," said Birdie.

"How about the other way around?" the sheriff said.

"What other way around?" said Mama, sounding annoyed. Not Grammy-level annoyance, but getting there.

"I'm just wondering if Birdie ever reached out to Drea," the sheriff said. "Sending her a letter, perhaps." He looked Birdie right in the eye. No problem! Birdie was great at looking dudes in the eye right back. Only this time she didn't, her gaze down at the table instead.

204

"How ridiculous!" Grammy said.

Mama nodded. "As if kids wrote letters these days. I doubt Birdie's ever written a letter in her life."

"Guess I'm out of it, as my own son never tires of telling me," the sheriff said. He smiled at Birdie. "Ever written a letter in your life, Birdie?"

Birdie gazed down at the table. She slowly shook her head.

"Of course not," said Mama. "I don't get the point of your question at all."

"My mistake," said the sheriff, his eyes on Birdie for a moment or two longer. Then he glanced at me, looked slightly surprised, maybe by how close to him I now seemed to be, my muzzle practically within touching distance of his calf. He shifted his leg away. "Back to this first meeting on the bridge, Birdie, if you don't mind. Drea drove up on her motorcycle and then . . . ?"

"She—"

The sheriff cut in. "Drea?"

Now Birdie did look up at him. Up and right in the eye. "Yeah, but I didn't know her name yet."

"Because they didn't know each other," Grammy said.

"Sorry," said the sheriff. "My mistake, if I haven't made that clear. Go on, Birdie."

"She," said Birdie, "asked about the catfish. We caught a catfish, me and Junior." She turned to Grammy. "Fifteen pounds six ounces—Snoozy weighed it."

"Then it could have been anything," Grammy said.

The sheriff shot her an annoyed look. We had a lot of annoyance going on in our kitchen, no idea why. "Go on," he said to Birdie.

"Then," Birdie began, and stopped. Her eyes shifted and she began again. "Then I guess was when she and Junior started talking about music. Junior's real interested in music and she—Drea—had a guitar case strapped to her motorcycle. She can write music so she invited us over to write down some of Junior's tunes."

"Over where?" the sheriff said.

"The campground," Birdie said.

"Mr. Santini's campground?" said Mama.

"Yeah."

"Did Bowser go, too?"

What a question! Where Birdie goes, I go. Didn't Mama know that by now?

"Yeah," Birdie said.

"I thought he hated dogs," Mama said. "And kids, for that matter."

"I don't think he does, Mama."

"Election coming up," said Grammy.

The sheriff changed how he was sitting in the chair, like he'd gotten uncomfortable. "Neither here nor there. What happened at the campground, Birdie?"

Birdie shrugged. "We went to her tent. She got out her guitar. She taught us a song—part of a song."

"What song?" the sheriff said.

"I don't know the name. It was about . . ." She looked around. ". . . being in a kitchen, nice and dry, out of the rain. She has . . ." Birdie's voice thickened. ". . . had a beautiful voice."

Then came a silence. I had no idea what anyone else was thinking, or if they were thinking at all. As for me, I was remembering the sound of Drea's voice. I have a real good memory when it comes to voices, can tell who's talking from far away.

"When did you discover that Drea was the daughter of the victim in your dad's last case?" the sheriff said.

Mama sat up straight. Her whole smell got sharper. It was still nice—Mama had a nice soapy smell, but now much . . . tangier, might be the way to put it.

"At the library," Birdie said. "There was a scrap of an old newspaper inside the guitar. I found the whole article at the library."

The sheriff gave her a long look. "This was after you saw her for the last time?"

Birdie nodded.

The sheriff rubbed his chin. I heard rasping sounds like he needed a shave.

"So she never discussed any of that with you?"

Birdie shook her head.

"What about the break-in? Did she mention that?"

"No."

Grammy tapped the side of her glass with her finger-nail. "Where are you going with this, Sheriff?"

"I'm just trying to piece things together," he said.

"Like what?" Mama said. "Don't you already know the drowning was accidental?"

"Miz Gaux here"—Sheriff Cannon nodded toward Grammy—"has clarified my thinking on that. Accidental or on purpose would be more like it. Just not murder. That doesn't mean I'm happy to leave things with a lot of loose ends."

Birdie looked at him closely. Loose ends? Where had I heard that before?

"But I understand this has been a lot for a kid to go through," the sheriff went on, "so if you'll please allow me one last question." His eyes were on Grammy but Grammy said nothing. It was Mama who gave him the nod.

"Thank you," he said. "Now, Birdie, did Drea ever say anything to you about a blog called *Kramer's Kold Kases*?"

Birdie thought. I could tell she was thinking by how her forehead, normally so smooth, wrinkled up. Also, I could feel her thoughts, kind of like dark birds flapping slowly through the room. That part was a bit scary so I forgot it at once.

"Yeah," Birdie said. "I think she mentioned it."

"In what context?"

"Context?" said Birdie. "I don't understand."

"Context," the sheriff said. "Well, uh . . ."

"Like what was being discussed at the time," Mama said, her voice low and gentle.

"Just about cold cases and what he said about them," Birdie said.

"What who said?" asked the sheriff.

"My daddy." Birdie turned to him. "You told us yourself—about warming up cold cases."

"That I did. And this one's sure warmed up, unless I'm way off track. This one, or maybe even these two."

"What do you mean?" Mama said.

"Nothing yet," said the sheriff. "Getting ahead of myself. My apologies."

"You've apologized enough, to my way of thinking," Grammy said. "How about some plain talk? Are you telling us that you're closing in on the killer of my son? You have some suspect after all these years?"

"No, ma'am. But something's been going on. If Drea said anything about *Kramer's Kold Kases*, it might be very helpful."

"All Ks," said Birdie.

"Excuse me?" the sheriff said.

"That was all she told me about *Kramer's Kold Kases*."

"Proves she knew about it, at least," the sheriff said. "Either of you ever heard of *Kramer's Kold Kases*?"

Mama and Grammy shook their heads.

"It's a blog devoted to cold cases, as you'd expect from the name," the sheriff said. "I did some quick looking into it. Seems to be a one-man operation run out of an old folks' home in Durango, Colorado, by a retired cop. Kind of a hobby for him, is my guess. He researches cold cases all over the U.S. and Canada, writes them up on his blog. I wouldn't call it a popular blog—my IT guy tells me it gets maybe a hundred hits a week, something like that. That's by way of background, point being that about a month ago this old blogger posted a write-up about Captain Gaux. From this little talk we're having it's now just about one hundred percent sure that Drea Bolden read that post. Most of it was pretty straightforward, nothing new, excepting one small detail that hasn't come up before."

"What detail?" Mama said.

"Are you familiar with a notebook your husband carried around with him?"

Mama's forehead wrinkled up, much the way Birdie's did, except that Mama had some wrinkles there all the time—faint, but there. "Vaguely," she said.

"Did you ever see it after?"

"*After* meaning after Robert's death?"

"Correct."

"I don't believe so. But why? What's this about?"

"Seems the Kold Kases guy has done some digging regarding that notebook."

Suddenly, I was all ears. Well, not really, although I've got some serious ears on me, compared to you, for example. But had digging entered the conversation? If so, I really hoped that if there was digging to be done everyone understood who was going to be doing it. Namely me, ol' Bowser.

"And he found an old sergeant down at the NOPD who remembered that Captain Gaux used to jot down thoughts about what he was working on in a little notebook," the sheriff was saying. Uh-oh. Had I missed something important? "Nothing fancy, just the ordinary kind of notebook you'd get at the five-and-dime. So the question is this: What became of the notebook?"

"No idea," Mama said.

"First I've heard of it," said Grammy.

The sheriff nodded. "It seems to have disappeared. According to this sergeant, if anybody had thought about it at the time, they'd probably have concluded it was lost in the river. Due to where the bod—the circumstances of where the death occurred, and all." The sheriff reached into his pocket, unfolded a sheet of paper. "I printed out the blog post. Seems this old blogger is of the opinion that there are other possibilities. I'll just read what he says." The sheriff put on a pair of glasses.

Whoa! He looked almost like a different person. That was bothersome. I got gripped by a strong desire to do some gnawing on the kitchen table leg. Almost certainly a no-no, so therefore I barely moved in that direction. Hardly at all. You'd never have noticed.

" 'Supposing the notebook didn't end up at the bottom of the Mighty Mississip,' he writes. 'What if—' "

"Mighty Mississip?" Grammy said.

The sheriff looked up. "I'm afraid that's his writing style ma'am, sorry." His gaze returned to the sheet of paper. " 'What if Captain Gaux was closing in on the killer of Henry Bolden? What if there's stone-cold proof in that notebook? What if he knew he himself was in danger and therefore put the notebook somewhere safe in the event that if things ended up exactly how they did end up, he'd have at least left an insurance policy out there? What if, what if, what if? All you readers out there in blogville? Where is the last notebook of Captain Robert Lee Gaux?' "

The sheriff took off his glasses and looked up.

seventeen

DOES THIS MEAN MY DAD...MY DAD'S body—was in the Mississippi River?" Birdie said.

Mama nodded.

Birdie's voice rose. Hey! She was angry! That upset me. I went over and sat on her feet, my only idea. "Why am I just finding this out now?"

"You never asked, Birdie," Mama said. "I made a decision to hold off on the details—the upsetting details—until the day you did ask. If that was wrong, I'm sorry."

Grammy folded her arms across her chest. "Told you it was wrong from the get-go."

Mama shot Grammy a sharp look, got one right back. I didn't like the way things were going, had a notion to gnaw on my tail.

"But the body of Drea's dad was in the river, too," Birdie said.

"That was noted at the time, Birdie," the sheriff said, "although there was a period of almost a month between the two . . . events. Plus there were other differences."

"Like?" Birdie said.

"Your father's body was found four or five miles up the river from Mr. Bolden's," the sheriff said. "And Mr. Bolden had been shot multiple times, whereas your father . . . your father had succumbed in a different manner."

"I don't understand."

The sheriff cleared his throat. "Head trauma."

"Trauma? I don't know that word. What does it mean?"

The adults looked from one to another, waiting for one to step up. Meanwhile, Birdie's eyes got moist and blurry.

"Injury," Mama said softly. "Bad injury."

"Like what kind of injury?" Birdie said.

There was a silence. Finally Sheriff Cannon said, "Shot in the back of the head. Close range—as though the killer had snuck up on him."

Birdie wiped her eyes with the back of her hand. At the same time she seemed to get hot. I could feel the heat rising off her.

"Getting back to these notebooks," the sheriff began, "is it—"

Grammy interrupted. "I don't know about any notebooks."

"You never saw him writing in one?" the sheriff said.

"No, sir," said Grammy.

"And you, ma'am?" the sheriff said, turning to Mama.

"I'm not sure. Maybe once or twice. But Robert did his best not to bring work home."

The sheriff's eyes shifted, like he was having some new thought. "That sounds wise," he said. He laid the sheet of paper on the table, smoothed it with his big hand. "Home meaning New Orleans, I take it."

"That's right," Mama said. "We lived in the Marigny back then, before it got so expensive."

"Did he ever say anything about what he was working on?" the sheriff said.

"Not never," said Mama. "But it was rare."

"What about the Bolden case?"

Mama shook her head. "The only case he mentioned in those last days before . . . in those last days, was something about birds."

"Birds?" said the sheriff.

"He said something about visiting a crazy old bird-watcher. Maybe it wasn't a case at all."

"Maybe not," said the sheriff. "When was the last time he was here?"

"I'd have to think," said Mama. "But probably the Fourth of July weekend that year. We always—we used to go out on the bayou and shoot fireworks off the deck of *Bayou Girl*. Birdie was just starting to talk that last time. She loved the fireworks. She kept yelling mo' mo' mo'. *Mo'* being one of her very first words."

What was this? Mama saying there was a time Birdie didn't know how to talk? I wasn't buying it. Birdie was the very best talker I'd ever come across, no one else even close.

"I remember that night," Grammy said. "We also snagged the prop on something and Robert had to swim down under the boat and free it. But—but that wasn't the last time he was here in St. Roch."

"No?" said the sheriff.

"He stopped in the day before he died," Grammy said.

"He did?" said Mama. "I never knew that."

"Kind of lost in all the . . . the turmoil of that time," said Grammy. "Plus I didn't see him—it was a spur-of-the-moment thing on his part. He was in Lafayette for a meeting or some such and ended up with a free hour or two. But I happened to be out with a customer at the time, so I missed him."

"Then how do you know this?" the sheriff said.

"On account of he left me a note, is how," Grammy said. "Plus some flowers." Her eyes got a faraway look. "Purple bellflowers." She took a deep breath, got rid of the faraway look. "Always been a favorite of mine. You used to find them by the Cleoma road willy-nilly, before they widened it."

"He left these things—the note and the flowers—over at the store?" the sheriff said.

"Who said anything about the store?" Grammy said. "I'm talking about right here, in this very room. Back then I lived in this part of the house, t'other side just for storage."

"I see," the sheriff said. "Was someone here to let him in?"

"Whatever for?" Grammy said. "Robert had a key."

The sheriff nodded. He thought. I could feel his thoughts, much darker and heavier than Birdie's. "Have there been any other break-ins?" he said.

"Other break-ins?" said Grammy.

"Besides the recent one," the sheriff said. "Over the years, meaning the time between that last visit of Captain Gaux's and now? And if not an actual break-in, then any suspicious activity around the house?"

"Nope," Grammy said. "What are you getting at?"

"Just gathering facts, is all," said the sheriff.

Which was when Birdie spoke, her voice so quiet it was more like just moving her lips. "He's making a theory of the case."

Everyone turned to her. "What was that?" said the sheriff, his voice way too sharp, in my opinion. I liked most humans and it's not that I disliked the sheriff, more that I'd never been sure of him. Were we headed toward some sort of dustup, me and him? Bring it on! I happened to notice I was no longer sitting on Birdie's feet.

The sheriff glanced down at me. The fact was I appeared to be rather close to his calf again, a big, muscular calf that might be fun to sink my—but no! Was that any way to behave? For a second or two, the sheriff's eyes filled with alarm. He shifted his leg well out of reach. No harm done!

Birdie looked up, spoke a little louder. "You're making a theory of the case."

"That's right," the sheriff said.

"Well then—out with it," said Grammy.

The sheriff shook his head. "It's too soon."

Mama spoke up. "How is that fair, Sheriff? You come here to collect facts and we do our best to help, but it's been a one-way street so far."

The sheriff gazed at Mama, and not in the friendliest way.

"Election coming up, Mr. Cannon," Grammy said, making the mister part stand out.

The sheriff whipped around toward her. He glared at Grammy, now looking real angry. Grammy glared right back. Did the sheriff think he could beat Grammy in a glaring contest? Grammy was the heavyweight glaring champion of the world! And maybe the sheriff realized that, because all of a sudden he started laughing.

"Something funny?" Grammy said.

The sheriff got himself under control, shook his head. "No, ma'am." He put his hands together, the way humans do when they're praying, whatever that is, praying being a complete mystery to me. "Theories of the case aren't something you want to jump into too fast." He glanced at Birdie. "Don't want to hitch yourself to the wrong wagon."

Wrong wagon? This was interesting. I'd seen one of my kind pulling a wagon on TV and had wanted to take a crack at it myself ever since. Imagine me pulling Birdie along in a wagon, faster and faster and faster! There's no getting better than that. Was today the day? I went on high alert.

"But," the sheriff went on, "sometimes it's hard to resist. A theory starts suggesting itself and won't wait. So here's what I'm thinking so far. Drea Bolden's arrival in our town and the break-in at nineteen Gentilly Lane are related."

The sheriff sat back, waiting for everybody to take in what he'd just said. If he was waiting for me to take it in, too, then we'd be here for some time. But in fact, Birdie spoke almost right away, her face amazed, and not in a good way.

"You're saying Drea did the break-in?"

"You yourself said Drea was aware of *Kramer's Kold Kases*, Birdie. I've had the opportunity to make a few calls down to New Orleans in the last hour or so, including one to her seventh-grade teacher—Drea was in seventh grade when her dad was murdered. According to the teacher, Drea had been a model kid until then, but she went off the rails. I won't go into all of that. What's important is that she became unstrung and never got restrung. And part of what ate away at her—a big part—was the not knowing." The sheriff glanced at Mama. "Not knowing the details, plus the fact that the killer or killers were still out there." Mama looked down. "So along comes *Kramer's Kold Kases* and this post about a missing notebook and the answers that might be in it. We're dealing with a very impulsive individual. She hops on her bike, breaks into Nineteen Gentilly Lane, and hunts around."

"She thought the notebook was here?" Mama said, glancing around the kitchen.

"What a load of nonsense!" said Grammy.

"Why couldn't she have just asked us?" Birdie said.

"I'm not saying it's a proven theory," the sheriff said. "It's a working theory."

"But there was a horrible mess," Birdie said. "Drea wouldn't have done it that way."

"No?" said the sheriff. "What about how she treated the guitar? Frustrated people do violent things."

"Meaning she didn't find the notebook?" Mama said.

"No godforsaken notebook to be found," Grammy said.

"Correct, at least the part about not finding the notebook," the sheriff said. "After that—the complete crushing of her hopes—I think Drea fell into despair and took herself down to Mr. Santini's pond."

There was a long silence. The sheriff rose soundlessly, like he was afraid of waking somebody. He put on his hat, touched the brim, opened the door, and went outside. We all stayed where we were, kind of strangely frozen in place. Then Birdie got up, walked quickly across the room and out the door. I followed, although by the time we came to the door I was in the lead. That was the first normal thing that had happened for some time.

We caught up to the sheriff as he was getting into his cruiser, one foot already inside. "Yes, Birdie?" he said. "Something I can do for you?"

"What about the other break-in?" Birdie said. "At the Richelieus'?"

"What about it?"

"Well, you said they were connected. The two break-ins, I mean. So are you saying Drea did the Richelieu break-in, too?"

Sheriff Cannon gazed down at her. When he spoke his voice was gentle but his eyes were not. Humans could be tricky at times—never their best times, in my opinion. "What are you up to, Birdie?"

Birdie backed away.

"I'm on your side," the sheriff said. "But I don't like to see a young lady disappointing her family."

Birdie's face turned bright red. I could feel the heat rising off her again. Was she mad at the sheriff? Because he was tricky? That was as far as I could take it. But if Birdie was mad, then wasn't it my job to be mad, too? I tried to make myself mad, found it a bit slowgoing.

"I—I would never do that," Birdie said. "They're the most—" Sometimes the human voice breaks in the middle of something they're saying, which I think was what happened to Birdie at that moment.

"Would they want you to lie to an officer of the law?" the sheriff said.

"I'm not lying to you!"

"There's lying and there's not coming clean. Real close to the same thing, the way I see it."

"Not coming clean? You're saying I'm not coming clean about something?"

"About your relationship with Drea Bolden. I think she got in touch with you long before she came here to St. Roch. I think there were letters back and forth. I think you let her know when nobody would be home at Nineteen Gentilly

Lane. And I think that after the break-in you did things to cover your tracks."

Birdie's eyes and mouth opened wide, like she was totally blown away. "But that—that's crazy!"

"You're calling me crazy?"

"None of what you said happened! It's all wrong!"

"Maybe some of the details need fixing," the sheriff said. "But these aren't just a bunch of wild suppositions on my part. I've got some proof."

"Proof? Proof of what?"

"I've seen some interesting video recently," the sheriff said. "Did you know there's twenty-four-hour video surveillance down at the post office?"

Birdie backed up another step.

"You made a brief appearance the other day. The camera wasn't aimed at a perfect angle, but from what I saw I believe you'd changed your mind about some letter you'd sent to Drea and concocted a plan to intercept it en route. A plan involving mail theft, by the way, which is a serious crime. But I'm willing to forget about that if you play ball. You can start by telling me about that letter."

"You want me to come clean?" Birdie said, backing away some more, her voice rising and rising. "You want me to come clean?"

Oh, how upset she was! I couldn't bear it. All I knew was that the sheriff had upset her and it was my job to stop him and stop him now. Suddenly, it was real easy to be mad. I felt my lips curling back all on their own, giving my teeth—big and sharp, in case you didn't know that yet—plenty of room to operate. Who knows what would have happened next? An episode with lots of red in it, that's for sure. But there was no red episode, because Birdie wheeled around and raced into the house, me right beside her.

We zoomed through the kitchen, now empty, and hurried into our bedroom. Birdie closed the door and grabbed her desk chair. In no time at all, she'd placed it on the bed, climbed up, and fished the rolled-up photo of Miranda Richelieu and her pearls out of the ceiling vent. Then—zoom—we flew back down the hall and out the door. We were moving and moving fast, which is when we're at our best, me and Birdie. As for why we were moving and moving fast, I had no idea. But did it even matter? What mattered were Birdie, me, and speed.

The sheriff was standing by his cruiser now, eyes on us, maybe looking a bit confused. Birdie went right up to him and handed—no. No, you couldn't say she handed the photo to Sheriff Cannon. More like she thrust it at him! Then she said, "Don't you whup Rory!"

Did the sheriff seem to tip backward a bit? I couldn't be sure, because we were already on the run again, back into the house. Birdie slammed the door.

From down the hall came Mama's voice. "Birdie? What's going on?"

"Nothing," Birdie said.

eighteen

AMA KNOCKED ON OUR DOOR. HUMANS
all have different knocks. Grammy's wasn't
the loudest I'd ever heard but it was the sharpest. Mama's was softer, although her hands were very strong.
For example, down at the store recently, Snoozy was having
trouble opening a jar of peanut butter and Mama had
unscrewed the top just like that. As for me and my kind, we
don't knock on doors. Clawing gets the job done for us.

"Birdie?" Mama called through the door. "You all right?"

"Yeah," said Birdie.

"Can I come in?"

"Sure." Birdie took the chair off the bed, put it in its
place by the desk.

Mama came in. She looked around. "Such a lovely little
room. Do you remember when we painted those clouds on
the wall?"

"Yeah."

"That was a fun day." Mama sat on the edge of the bed.
Birdie leaned against the desk. I sat beside Birdie, or possibly in front of her, maybe even somewhat on her feet.

226

"How are you?" Mama said.

"Me?" said Birdie. "Fine."

"This is all so upsetting. I know I'm upset, and Grammy, too. So you must be, as well."

Birdie nodded.

"No need to be a stoic around me, sweetheart. Say what's on your mind."

"What's a stoic?"

"Someone who just sucks it up."

"Was my dad a stoic?" Birdie said.

"I'd have to say yes."

"Around you?"

Mama tilted her head, like she was trying to see Birdie from a different angle. I sometimes do the same thing. "You mean when it was just the two of us together?"

"Yeah."

Mama looked past Birdie, gazed at our wall—meaning Birdie's and mine—the sky-blue wall dotted with puffy white clouds. "No, he shared with me," Mama said. She turned to Birdie. "But never in a complaining way, that's true."

"Is that like a family thing?" Birdie said. "Not complaining?"

"Kind of," Mama said. "But it's not complaining to have a real discussion about what we just heard from the sheriff. So let's hear what you've got to say."

"You first," Birdie said.

Mama laughed. "Fair enough." Her face got real serious. "Here's what I've got to say. Whatever investigations you've been doing—or you and your new buddy Junior Tebbets—must stop now. First there's the break-in, and now this horrible death of a strange young woman—"

"She wasn't strange!"

"—who seems to have taken an interest in you for reasons I don't understand. So until the sheriff clears all this up, put that curiosity of yours on the back burner."

"But the sheriff's wrong about Drea! No way she ever would have broken into our house."

"How do you know?"

"I just do. And not just that, but the other thing, too. About . . . about despair and going in the pond and all that."

"Then let the sheriff discover that for himself."

"But will he? Is he a good sheriff? That's what's on my mind, Mama."

"He's a good man, as far as I can tell."

"But is he good at his job? What did my dad think?"

"Mr. Cannon was still a deputy then, and we were down in the city, so we didn't see him much."

"I hear a *but*," Birdie said.

Mama laughed. "Okay, okay. Rob—your dad—once said that Mr. Cannon had a tendency to jump to conclusions.

Rob believed in resisting conclusions, making them come to him."

"I don't get it."

"Neither did I, really," Mama said. "I wish—"

Grammy poked her head in the doorway. "Told her yet?"

"I was getting to it," Mama said. "First I wanted to—"

"Told me what?" said Birdie.

Mama sighed. "All right," she said. "Birdie, we've received an offer on the house."

"Huh?" said Birdie.

"On this house," Mama said. "Our house. Someone has offered to buy it, offered a very good price."

"Far more than it's worth," Grammy said. "Unless we're sitting on a diamond mine, which we most surely are not."

"Maybe more than it's worth to us, but not to him," Mama said.

"To who?" said Birdie. "What's going on? I don't understand."

"And," Mama went on, still talking to Grammy, "with the extra money we'll be able to buy a nicer place. Maybe even build our own house—there's a lot for sale in Hilltop Estates."

"Pah," said Grammy.

"Doesn't have to be Hilltop Estates," Mama said. She

gave Grammy one of those pointed looks. "Although it is gated. In any case, we'd be free to—"

"You're selling our house?" Birdie said.

"Nothing's definite yet," Mama said.

"But—but why? I love our house! Are we having, like, money problems?" Birdie went still. "This is because of losing your—of what happened at your job, isn't it?"

"No, no," Mama said. "It's—"

Grammy cleared her throat in a very loud way. In fact, it was the loudest throat clearing I'd ever heard, reminding me of the machine shop across the bayou from Gaux Family Fish and Bait.

Mama whipped around toward her. "Please! This is hard enough."

"Very well," Grammy said, backing into the hall. "But there are ulterior motives at play, sure as shootin'."

Grammy moved off down the hall. Mama turned back toward Birdie.

"I don't want you worrying about money. I've got three interviews next week and they all look promising."

"For the same kind of job as before?"

"Maybe not quite the same, but plenty good enough. The point is this offer that's come in for the house could really change our situation."

"How much is the offer?"

Mama said some complicated number, too hard for me to follow.

"That's a lot, huh?" Birdie said.

"Sure is," said Mama.

"You really want to live in a gated community, Mama?"

"I'm starting to think there's a lot to be said for it."

Birdie was quiet for a moment or two. "Who's the person?" she said.

"The person who wants to buy?" Mama licked her lips, like they'd gone dry. "It's Vin—Mr. Pardo."

"He . . . he wants to buy our house?"

"Most definitely."

"Doesn't he live in New Orleans?"

"Correct," said Mama. "But he wants to establish what he calls a beachhead here in St. Roch."

"Beachhead? We don't have beaches here, Mama."

Mama smiled. "A beachhead just means a point of entry, a place to get started. He wants to build a high-tech business in St. Roch, all about renting out time on these new servers he's buying in China."

"He's going to put a high-tech business in our house?"

Mama laughed. "The house will be where his initial team lives while they're getting the business set up. I think he's planning to build a sort of warehouse for the servers on that vacant land out past Hector's Ice Cream."

Birdie, still leaning against the desk, folded her arms. "What's 'ulterior motive'?"

"Oh, that." Mama's face got a bit pink. You saw pink on a lot on people's faces here in St. Roch—it was the hot time of year—although this particular pinkness seemed different. "An ulterior motive is when you say you have a reason for doing something but the real reason is something else."

Birdie thought about that. I did not. Why? Way too hard, that's why. "So," she said, "Mr. Pardo doesn't really want to do the servers thing?"

"Oh, boy," said Mama. "There it is again."

"There what is?"

"That laser in your brain—always zeroing in on the key question."

"Laser in my brain? I got mostly Bs this year."

"It's not about Bs," Mama said. "And it's way more important than Bs in the long run. Your dad had it, too. As for ulterior motives, Grammy thinks that Vin's main interest in buying the house is to help me out."

"Why would he want to do that?"

"He's a generous person and a very successful one. He likes giving back."

"Is that what Grammy thinks? It's because he's generous?"

"Ka-boom!" said Mama. "Laser strike! No, Birdie, that's not what Grammy thinks. But she's wrong. Vin is doing this for business reasons. The extra amount he's paying for the house is what he calls an inducement for us to sell when we had no previous plans to do that."

"Oh."

"So how do you feel about all this?"

Birdie put her hand between my ears and gave me a little scratch. How did she know I was itchy? I hadn't even known myself, not until she'd started scratching. Was this part of the laser thing in her mind, whatever that was all about? I had no idea, and didn't care. Birdie was the best scratcher in the whole swamp, end of story.

She looked up. "What happened to his head?"

"What are you talking about?"

"Mr. Pardo's forehead. He had a bandage on it."

"Oh, that," said Mama. "Bumped into an overhanging branch, I think he said. But you haven't answered my question. How do you feel about all this?"

"Do you like him?" Birdie said.

"He seems like a nice man."

"Does he like you?"

"I believe he does. But no one's in any hurry to . . . to be in any hurry. And a woman in my position has to be very sure in her mind."

"What position is that, Mama?"

"A position of, well, potential loneliness."

Birdie pushed away from the desk, walked over to Mama, and hugged her. "I don't want you to be lonely."

"Oh, I'm most certainly not." Mama patted Birdie's head. She was looking over Birdie's shoulder, in fact in my direction. "I have everything I'd ever want or need."

That sounded nice. But shouldn't the person saying it have looked happier about the whole thing? That was my only thought—one of the biggest I'd ever had. I let them hug for what seemed like ages before I squeezed in between. She's my Birdie, after all.

"And remember," Mama went on when I had them nicely separated. "Curiosity—back burner. That means no poking around by yourself."

"I've got Bowser," Birdie said, the most obvious thing I'd ever heard from her.

"Good thing," said Mama. "But the point is—no poking around."

Not long after that, we went for a walk, me and Birdie. Like most of our walks, this one began on the breezeway.

"Bowser! What are you growling about?"

That was easy: I was growling about the snake that lived under our breezeway, its scent particularly strong today. Also, I could hear it slithering around down there. Why? What was on its snaky mind? I did not want a snake living at 19 Gentilly Lane. Nineteen Gentilly Lane was just for me, Birdie, Grammy, and Mama. Actually, just me and Birdie would have been perfect.

"Bowser! Come!"

If Birdie calls, I go, maybe not immediately, but always eventually. You can take it to the bank.

We walked up Gentilly Lane. When we walk, me and Birdie, I like to be on the side closest to the road. That means that when we cross over to the other side, I have to do a sort of double crossover, a tricky move—

"Oof! Bowser!"

—that I've gotten pretty good at. Soon we came to a dirt road, cane fields stretching away on both sides, the air full of sugary breezes. How nice! We walked along side by side, not a care in the world.

"Oh, Bowser. I'm so worried."

Uh-oh. Did that mean we did have a care in the world? News to me, but if Birdie was worried I was worried. My tail slumped down right away, dragging along behind me. I got it back up to its proper place. You've got to show some pride in this world, or else . . . I couldn't think of the "or else," but I'm sure it's all about a very good reason for keeping your tail up.

"No poking around, but Drea would never do those things, Bowser. Like breaking into our house. And what about the break-in at the Richelieus'? Drea didn't even know the—" She stopped talking and stopped walking at the same time, one foot hovering for a moment above the ground. "Oh, no." She lowered her foot. "Remember when Drea asked if we'd seen a boat going under the bridge? And then later, when I mentioned about the pearls, she seemed pretty interested?"

I remembered none of those things, but since Birdie remembered I didn't have to. You really can't beat our arrangement.

"Did she know the Richelieus after all?" Birdie said. "Do I have to tell the sheriff? I don't want to see him, Bowser, not ever."

I was totally with her on that. So everything was cool. Meanwhile, the dirt road we were on had led us to the gate of Mr. Santini's campground. Mr. Santini was out front, a garden trowel in one hand and a pencil behind his ear. Birdie sometimes stashed gum behind her ear, still the coolest thing I'd ever seen in this life, but a pencil wasn't bad. I was starting to like Mr. Santini.

He was talking to an old man who stood leaning against the open door of a car. The old man was very thin, had a few thin strands of hair on top of his head, and seemed to be trembling a little bit. Because he felt cold? That was hard to believe on a day like this, but he did have his shirt buttoned right to the top.

Mr. Santini looked our way. "Birdie? What are you doing here?"

We drew closer. "I was wondering what happened to her things—like the tent and the motorcycle. Maybe her family should, um . . ."

"Problem being," said Mr. Santini, "Drea Bolden doesn't seem to have had much in the way of family. The sheriff's workin' on that, supposedly. Meanwhile, he's impounded all her stuff down at the station. This here"—Mr. Santini pointed the trowel at the old man—"is Mister—didn't quite catch your handle."

"Volk," said the old man in a thin old voice. "Sidney Volk."

"Mr. Volk, like you to meet Birdie Gaux, local girl who figured out where the body was." Mr. Santini turned to Birdie. "Mr. Volk is Drea's accountant, from down in New Orleans."

"Not exactly her accountant," Mr. Volk said. "I was her father's accountant. Now I'm retired." All this time he kept trembling. I wanted to help in some way, tried to think how. While I was getting nowhere with that, Mr. Volk looked my way. His eyes were washed-out like Grammy's, but her gaze had lots of force behind it and Mr. Volk's did not. "I had a dog like this one once. Think he'd let me pet him?"

"Bowser," Birdie said. "Go see Mr. Volk."

I went over to Mr. Volk. He reached out and patted my head with his cold, bony hand. His trembling seemed to die down a bit. We were a good team, me and Birdie.

"I was just explaining the whole story to Mr. Volk," Mr. Santini said. "He hadn't heard about her . . . being deceased and all. But I'm still not clear on the purpose of your visit, Mr. Volk. Like why you came all this way. If you don't mind my asking."

"Not too sure myself," Mr. Volk said, now just resting his hand on my head. "Don't know if you're aware that Henry Bolden—her father and my former client—was a real estate developer. Seems he had a safe-deposit box no one knew about till the bank got taken over last month. It contained only one document, which Ms. Bolden hired me to examine. I was unable to come to any conclusions. I called to tell her that a couple of days ago and she asked me to bring the document. Here I am."

"Hmm," said Mr. Santini. He tapped his potbelly with the tip of the trowel. "You say you have it on you, this document?"

"I do."

"Any chance I can take a quick gander?"

"I don't see why not," said Mr. Volk. He took a folded sheet of paper from an inside pocket of his suit jacket and handed it to Mr. Santini.

Mr. Santini unfolded the sheet of paper and looked it over. "Hmm," he said. "Would appear that just about ten years ago, Mr. Bolden made a personal loan for ninety-five thousand dollars."

"Appears that way," Mr. Volk said.

"To some outfit name of the Cardinal Fund."

"Correct. But there's no such entity registered with the state of Louisiana, then or now."

"Hmm," said Mr. Santini. "Did you know about this loan at the time?"

"I did not," Mr. Volk said. "But I only did the books for Mr. Bolden's business interests, not his personal accounting."

Then we just sort of stood around for a bit. A breeze sprang up, carrying the smell of Mr. Santini's pond. All of a sudden I wanted to go home.

"Ninety-five big ones, huh?" Mr. Santini said.

"According to the document," said Mr. Volk.

"And at an interest rate of thirty percent, says here." Mr. Santini looked up from the document. "That's a mobster-type number."

"Mr. Bolden was no mobster," said Mr. Volk. "Not in my dealings with him."

"There's them that have secret lives," Mr. Santini said. "Any evidence that the loan got repaid?"

"That was Ms. Bolden's question," Mr. Volk said. "I found no evidence of repayment. But of course the trail has grown sketchy after all this time."

"Hmm," said Mr. Santini, handing back the sheet of paper. Mr. Volk said good-bye, gave me one last pat, and drove away.

nineteen

INETY-FIVE THOUSAND DOLLARS IS A lot of money, Bowser," Birdie said as we walked back up the dirt road, away from the campground. "But what's it all about? What was Drea doing?"

I had nothing to offer on that one, but I was happy being away from the pond, far enough distant now that I could only smell it if I tried, which I did not. Except for once or twice. Funny how sometimes you can't stop yourself from doing something you already know has zero chance of working out!

"What is the Cardinal Fund? Was Drea's dad a bad guy?" Wow! Those sounded like tough questions, each and every one. "You know how Grammy says don't go stirring up a hornet's nest?" Birdie went on. "Maybe that's what Drea did."

Oh, no. Anything but hornets! Once I'd stepped on a hornet, completely by accident. Your poor paw doesn't forget things like that. I listened my hardest for the buzz of hornets, heard none. What I did hear was the pound-pound of human running footsteps. A few moments after that, a

241

runner came into view around a bend on the dirt road up ahead. He was a big guy—or maybe a big kid, of the teenage type—and he was a very fast runner. Not fast compared to me and my kind, but fast for a human. As the runner came closer, I saw that in fact he was a big kid of the teenage type, wearing gray sweats despite the heat. A big teenager with a broad face and heavy eyebrows, eyebrows that struck me as pushy. Hey! Did I know him?

"Preston Richelieu," Birdie said quietly. Yes, I knew him, all right: the dude who liked to make his hand into a gun and point it at us. Birdie veered over to the side of the road, giving him plenty of room. The distance between us and him closed fast. *Pound pound, pound pound.* I could feel Preston Richelieu's strength right through the ground. His hair flopped up and down, drops of sweat spraying into the air. They caught the light in a way I'd normally find beautiful, but right now—here on this dirt road, just the three of us—I did not.

Preston, in the middle of the road, pounded toward us, his gaze straight ahead. Most runners look like they're zoning out. Not Preston. He looked like he was annoyed about something. Was he annoyed with himself for wearing sweats—dark with moisture—on such a hot day? That was my only thought. We kept walking, me and Birdie, me in between her and the middle of the road. Preston's rapid breathing grew louder and louder, and then he zoomed past us, never once looking our way.

We walked on, me and Birdie, and—

Whoa. The pounding stopped, and so did the vibrations beneath my feet. I looked back, and there was Preston, no longer running. He was gazing at us, his big chest heaving.

"Hey!" he called.

Birdie turned and looked at him.

"Hey!" Preston said again. "You that Birdie kid?"

Birdie nodded.

"Thought so." Preston moved toward us. For one moment I thought Birdie was about to turn and run the other way, but she did not. And then it was too late.

Some humans stand a little too close, don't give you enough space. Preston turned out to be one of those. He stared down at Birdie, sweat dripping off his chin. The whole world seemed to smell of Preston's sweat, out there on the quiet dirt road between Mr. Santini's campground and the first houses in town.

"Know who I am?" he said.

"Preston Richelieu."

"That's right."

"Quarterback of the Hornets," Birdie said. Very softly, she added, "*Woo-woo*."

Whatever that was about, it might have been a mistake,

because Preston's face reddened and he loomed in even closer.

"You're a troublemaker," he said.

Birdie's lower lip quivered a bit. I could smell how afraid she was. But she didn't back away. Also, she stood very straight. She didn't speak, just shook her head in a quick little shake meaning No, I'm not a troublemaker.

Preston raised his hand and pointed his finger right in Birdie's face. Preston's finger was thick and strong and had dirt under the nail. "That's a lie. You're making trouble for my family."

"I'm not."

Preston's voice rose. "You are!"

Birdie was shaking now. This was bad. How about we end this chitchat and go our separate ways? I wondered how to make that happen, and came up with no answers.

Preston jabbed his finger at Birdie, got real close to actually touching her. His eyebrows, dark and thick, were all bunched up in a very agitated way. "You sure are! And if you don't stop you're gonna pay. Pay big-time."

"Your family," Birdie said, even softer than before, "made its own trouble."

Preston seemed to swell up and hover over us like a storm cloud. "What did you just say? What did you just say?"

My guess was that this would have been a good moment for silence on Birdie's part, and maybe she came close to keeping her mouth shut. But then, so quietly that even I could barely hear, she said, "What's the story with the pearls?"

Preston stabbed her with his finger, stabbed her real hard in the chest. Birdie gasped like she'd had the wind knocked out of her, lost her balance, and fell backward, landing on the road with a hard thump. Preston strode forward, stood over her, and lifted his foot like he was going to do something awful. She raised her hand—so small compared with Preston's foot—to protect herself. I saw red.

Redness took over my whole mind. I had no more thoughts. All I knew was that this red-minded Bowser was now in midair, springing at Preston full strength, nothing held back. And Bowser's a pretty big guy, don't forget, the kind of big guy who eats you out of house and home—just ask Grammy. Red-minded Bowser smashed into Preston's chest, knocking him away from Birdie. He staggered but didn't lose his balance, then yelled a wild yell, spun around in the sort of martial arts move you see on TV, and launched a kick at red-minded Bowser.

What he didn't appreciate was red-minded Bowser's speed. Which was why Preston ended up with his thigh caught between powerful jaws. Red-minded Bowser squeezed on those jaws and sank his big strong teeth into Preston's leg. Preston let out a high-pitched scream that seemed to fill the sky. Then, in a desperate sort of panic, he wriggled free and shot off down the road. Red-minded Bowser took off after him, nipping at his heels. Preston: real fast for a human, but red-minded Bowser wasn't going full speed, not even close.

"Get him away from me! Get him away from me!"

Like that was going to work. Preston ran and screamed. Red-minded Bowser ran and nipped. Then, from up ahead, meaning the direction of town, appeared a strange sight, namely an approaching kid, beating on a small drum hung around his neck. A skinny kid with a Mohawk? Yes. Had to be Junior Tebbets. His eyes widened in surprise, and were still widening when Preston ran right over him. Junior flew one way, his drumsticks another, and the drum a third. Red-minded Bowser got a bit confused. He gave Preston's heel one more nip—

"ARRGH!"

—and then turned back toward Junior, lying in the road. Red-minded Bowser stopped seeing red.

Junior sat up. "Bowser?" he said. "What's going on?"

Much too complicated to explain even if I'd had the ability, which I did not. But what a good mood I was in!

246

The taste of human blood? Not bad at all, if on the salty side. Still, probably best not to make this a habit. Perhaps just on special occasions.

Birdie came running up. "Oh, Bowser!" she said. "My hero!" She gave me a big kiss, right on the nose. My good mood got even better.

"Birdie?" Junior said. "What happened here? Was that Preston Richelieu?"

Birdie helped Junior to his feet. She started explaining things. He asked questions. She explained some more. All of this? Impossible to follow, at least for me. At the same time we picked up Junior's drum and one of the drumsticks, then started searching among the sugarcane stalks for the other one.

"What were you doing with the drum?" Birdie said.

"Taking it to the campground," Junior said. "I was going to sit out there by the pond and see if I could make up a song about Drea."

Birdie gave him a long look. "Good idea," she said.

"Thanks."

She poked around a cane stalk. "Here it is." She handed him the second drumstick. "Let's go home, Bowser."

"Maybe I'll come with you," Junior said. "Do the song on another day."

"Sure," said Birdie. "Let's go, my hero."

They started up the road.

"Meaning you, Bowser."

I took a step or two toward them, then stopped. What was that smell? Leather? One of my favorites. I nosed around the base of a cane stalk and found a small leather wallet. A sweaty wallet, and the sweat smelled of Preston. I picked it up anyway and brought it to Birdie.

"What did you find, Bowser?" she said, taking it from me.

"Looks like a wallet," said Junior. "Any money in it?"

"Even if there is it's not ours."

"That's one way of looking at it."

Birdie opened the wallet. "There's a driver's license."

"Let's see." Junior grabbed the wallet, took out the license. "Hey! It's Preston's."

"He must have lost it when he bumped into you," Birdie said.

"Bumped into? That's what you call it?" Junior gazed at the license. "One ugly dude," he said.

"Let's see." Junior handed Birdie the license. She looked at it. Her eyes widened. "His middle name is Pardo?"

"Huh?"

"Pardo," Birdie said. "Says it right here—Preston Pardo Richelieu. Oh my god!"

"What's so amazing?" said Junior. "I don't get it."

"How come his middle name is Pardo?"

"Parents must have given it to him."

Birdie said nothing, went on staring at the driver's license.

"For example, my middle name is Earl," Junior said. "What's yours?"

"This has to mean something," Birdie said. "Something important."

"A pretty long name," said Junior. "I'd stick to Birdie." Then he laughed and laughed, like he'd just said something very funny. Birdie didn't seem to get it or even notice.

"Pardo is his middle name," she said.

"I see that," said Junior. "An uncool name? Is that where you're going with this? Kind of sucks, now that I think of it—parents can stick an uncool name on you."

"But why?" Birdie said. "Why Pardo?"

Junior shrugged. "Is it a word? Like *birdie* is a little bird. Maybe Pardo's a little . . . something or other. How about we ask him?"

"Ask Preston?"

"Or maybe you ask him. When you return the wallet. Um, if that's in your plans. There is such a thing as finders keepers."

"I don't think finders keepers is part of the law."

"Gotta be," said Junior. "What else is in there?"

Birdie looked through the wallet. "A credit card."

"He's got a credit card?"

"Gold American Express. And there's money, too. Looks like . . . a hundred and twenty dollars."

"He walks around with a hundred and twenty dollars? And a gold card?"

Birdie checked the license. "He is seventeen years old, Junior."

"No way .I'll have all that when I'm seventeen," Junior said.

"How do you know?"

" 'Cause his family's rich and mine's not, that's how. Is your family rich, Birdie?"

"No. But that doesn't mean I'm stuck in not being rich forever."

"You want to be rich?"

"I actually haven't thought about it," Birdie said. "And I don't have time." She held up the wallet. "Plus what am I going to do about this?"

"Keep it, like I said. I won't tell."

"I'm not keeping it, but I don't want to see Preston anytime soon."

"You could drop it off at the police station," Junior said. "Lost and found."

Birdie thought about that. Meanwhile, Junior dusted off

his drum, slung it over is neck. He tapped on it with the sticks, light and slow. *Tap, tap-tap-tap.*

"Maybe I'll head down to the pond after all. I kinda feel a song coming, a song about Drea. You in?"

Birdie shook her head.

Junior gazed down the road. "Think she committed suicide, like they say?"

"No," said Birdie.

"You did good, Bowser," Birdie said when we were alone, walking back into town, Junior having continued on toward the campground. "Real, real good. What would I do without you?"

That was an easy question. The answer was that we didn't even have to think about it. Birdie and I were going to be together forever. Ask me a tough one, Birdie!

But there were no more questions. We headed into town, soon found ourselves standing outside the police station. It stood across a little square from the post office and looked pretty much the same, as if they'd both been built from the same pile of rust-colored bricks. Birdie's hand was in the pocket of her shorts, wrapped around Preston's wallet. I could smell the leather and also the sweat on her hand, now mixed with Preston's sweat. I didn't like that part of it.

Birdie gazed at the blue light above the police station door, dim and weak in the sunshine. "This could go wrong, Bowser," she said.

Uh-oh. A problem? What kind of problem could worry us? Hadn't we just taken down Preston, a pretty big dude, after all? I'd nipped at his heels and he'd yelled his head off: Life doesn't get much better than that. I wondered who else's heels might be nippable, thought at once of the sheriff. I was having a real good day.

"How could it go wrong?" Birdie continued. "I don't know. It's just a feeling. Has the sheriff gone to the Richelieus' place with that photo? Is that how come Preston was so mad? But that would mean the sheriff told them who gave him the photo! How can we ever trust him?"

The door of the police station opened and out stepped Officer Perkins, licking a green Popsicle. It looked so cool and refreshing. I wanted it pretty bad.

He saw us and paused. Officer Perkins was a huge dude, way bigger than Preston. I studied his heels. He wore black leather shoes, highly polished.

"Hi, Birdie," he said.

"Hi." She jammed her hand deeper into her pocket.

"Looking for the sheriff?"

"No."

"He should be back real soon."

"We're just . . . just out for a walk."

"Hot day for walking," Perkins said. "Anything I can help you with?"

"No," said Birdie. "No, thanks. Come, Bowser." We moved off.

"If you change your mind . . ." Perkins called after us.

We kept going, didn't look back. The rumble of his deep voice stayed with me even after he'd spoken. Soon we were on a little street that ran along the bayou and led to one end of Gentilly Lane. It was a nice, shady street with a café and a restaurant or two overlooking the water.

"Let's go home and ask Mama what to do," Birdie said. "It's the only thing I can think—"

She went silent. Up ahead was the café. Was Trixie's the name? I thought so. We often passed it but never went in. "Three bucks for a cup of coffee?" Grammy said. "What world are they living in?" Trixie's had a table outside, overhung with an umbrella. Two people sat at the table, a man and a woman. He said something that made her laugh. He laughed, too, then briefly laid his hand on top of hers. Mama was the woman. The man was Vin Pardo.

twenty

WE CAME TO A HALT. OR RATHER, Birdie came to a halt and as soon as I saw that, I did the same thing. So there we were, standing still, not more than a few steps away from Trixie's Café by the bayou. How come we weren't walking up to the table where Mama sat with Pardo and saying, "Hi, Mama, how's it going?" or something of that nature? I had no idea. In fact, we seemed to be shrinking backward, like we were about to slip away and take some other route. Meanwhile, the fur on my back was doing that iron-spike thing.

"Oh, before I forget," Pardo said, "here's the deposit check." He handed Mama a little slip of paper. "Slightly postdated—just a technicality." Mama moved to take the check, and that was when she caught sight of us.

"Birdie?" she said.

"Hi," said Birdie. She jammed her hand deep into her pocket, the pocket that held Preston's wallet.

Pardo turned our way. For the very briefest moment he did not look happy to see us. Then his whole face changed in a flash to very, very happy. That bothered me, but what bothered me even more was what he had sitting in his lap. Namely, a cat. Not just any cat, but the golden-colored cat I'd first seen that early morning—everyone still asleep but me—when Pardo had driven slowly past our house. Bonnie was the name of this cat, unless my memory was playing tricks on me, which was always a possibility. She arched her back up in a lazy sort of stretch and gave me a lazy sort of look, a look that said, "What's your excuse?" Or something even nastier. We were not going to be friends. That was clear from the get-go.

"Well, well," Pardo said. "Hello there, Birdie. Summer days are dragging by now, I'll bet."

"Dragging?" said Birdie.

"I remember just itching to go back to school by the end of summer, when I was your age. And I was no big fan of school, believe me."

"This was in New Orleans?" Birdie said.

Pardo blinked. "Why, yes. New Orleans."

"Everything all right, Birdie?" Mama said.

"Yeah."

"You look . . . a little funny. And why is Bowser growling like that?"

Growling? Me? I listened and yes, thought I detected nearby growling. Maybe Mama was right. I did what I could to get it under control.

"Reacting to Bonnie, I expect," Pardo said. "Here,

Bonnie, go on over and make friends with the ugly-looking brute over there." He sort of tossed Bonnie down onto the sidewalk. She landed in an easy, flexible way, like she could safely jump off tall buildings if she had to. Had I ever met anyone more annoying? Bonnie took another lazy look at me and glided right back up on Pardo's lap. He laughed and stroked her golden back. She purred, perhaps not in the least a loud or harsh sound, but it hurt my ears big-time.

"Bowser's not ugly," Birdie said.

"'Course not," Pardo said. "Just an expression." He stroked Bonnie's back. "I guess I was projecting what was on Bonnie's mind."

"And Birdie was doing the same thing with Bowser," Mama said, with a little laugh.

Pardo laughed, too. "Don't we all do that with pets?"

"He's the best-looking dog in the whole town," Birdie said.

Pardo held up his hands. "Hey! I surrender!" Then his gaze fell on Birdie's pocket, the one she had her hand jammed in, and his eyes narrowed. Just for an instant, but Mama caught it, and looked in the same direction.

"What's that in your pocket?" she said. "A treat for Bowser, is my guess."

A very nice guess on Mama's part. I really wished it was true.

"Um," said Birdie, taking her hand out of her pocket but then kind of not knowing what to do with it. Meanwhile, the outline of a square-shaped object was pretty clear against the fabric of her shorts.

"Funny-shaped treat," Pardo said.

"It is," said Mama. "Now I'm curious, Birdie."

Pink blotches spread across Birdie's cheeks. How nervous she smelled! I tried to think how to make her less nervous but came up empty. I moved closer to her side, all I could think of to do.

"It's not a treat," she said, looking not into Mama's eyes, instead sort of at her chin. "More like a . . . uh, a wallet. I found a wallet. It, ah, belongs to Snoozy. It's Snoozy's wallet!"

"Goodness," said Mama. "Where did you find it?"

"I'm on my way to the store to give it to him right now," Birdie said. "Come on, Bowser!"

She took a step and part of the next one before Mama said, "But wherever did you find it?"

"Oh, just on the . . . porch. At the store, more like in the parking lot."

"But why didn't you go in the store and give it to him then?"

"He—he wasn't there. He'd gone out. For a snack. A quick snack with . . . with his uncle Lem."

Mama tilted her head, gave Birdie a questioning sort of look. Pardo sat back in his chair, elbows on the armrests.

"A quick snack with Uncle Lem?" Mama said. "No such thing."

"Ha-ha." Birdie laughed, but not her usual laugh at all. This was high-pitched and almost unpleasant, Birdie incapable of making any sounds that were truly unpleasant. "Well, bye!" she said, and started walking quickly away, me right with her. I felt eyes on us until we rounded a bend on the bayou walk and Gaux Family Fish and Bait came into view.

"Oh, Bowser, I messed that up so bad."

Birdie messing something up? I had no idea what she was talking about.

"I lied to Mama," she said. "Lied and lied and lied."

She had? Not that I'd noticed. What was lying all about, again? I tried to get my mind around it. And gave up pretty quick. Some parts of the human world are so complicated it's best not to even go there.

"But what could I do?" Birdie went on, as we approached the back entrance of the store. "What if I'd told her whose wallet it really was? With Mr. Pardo right there? And Preston's middle name being Pardo? How could I let that happen? Doesn't whatever's going on—Drea, her dad, my dad—connect to the name Pardo? But how, Bowser? How?"

Whoa! So many questions! I preferred to take questions one at a time. Actually, none at a time. We climbed the back steps, Birdie pushing a crab trap aside with her foot, and entered Gaux Family Fish and Bait.

Snoozy sat by the cash register, head on the counter, drooling slightly. What a face Snoozy had at that moment! Not a care in the world. How would it be to live Snoozy's life? Not bad, not bad at all! Once, he and I had shared one of my biscuits. Let's keep that between you and me.

"Snoozy?" Birdie said. "Snoozy?"

Snoozy groaned, shifted his head slightly, made a contented sound, and went back to what he'd been doing, namely enjoying a nap.

"Snoozy!"

He slept on. Birdie stepped up to the counter and—and gave that counter a smack! Wow! Just like Grammy, although not quite so hard.

Snoozy's head snapped up. "Wasn't sleeping, boss, just resting my eyes for a—Oh. It's you." He rubbed his eyes. "Hey! Is it true about that motorcycle girl from New Orleans? She committed suicide?"

"It's true she's dead," Birdie said.

"Wow. And just the other day she was standing in this very store, right where you are, in fact."

Birdie glanced at the door. "Listen, Snoozy. We may not have much time."

"For what?"

"To get our stories straight."

"Stories? Like about how I wasn't really sleeping, just resting my eyes? Which happens to be the truth. I have the kind of eyes that need a lot of rest—school nurse told me that way back when. But your grammy don't believe me and she swore she was going to can my butt the next time—"

"Snoozy!" For a moment I thought Birdie was about to give the counter another smack, but she did not. "Forget about sleep for once."

"For once? That's not very nice, Birdie. And here I always thought that you and me—"

"Sorry," Birdie said, taking a deep breath. "This isn't about sleep or Grammy—Hey! Where is she?"

"Out with a customer on *Bayou Girl*."

"I wish—" Birdie began, and then stopped herself. "This isn't about sleep or Grammy or anything like that. It's about your wallet."

"Oh, no. Don't tell me I lost it again!" Snoozy patted his pockets.

"That's exactly it!" Birdie said. "You lost your wallet."

"Huh? But here it is." He pulled a worn-looking wallet from one of his pockets and held it up.

"Right," Birdie said. "You have it now. But you lost it and I found it and gave it back to you."

"When was this?"

"Never, Snoozy! That's what I'm trying to tell you. I found another wallet but if anyone asks, you say I found yours."

"Whose wallet didja find?"

"That's not the point. The point is—"

"Yeah, except what do I say when they ask whose wallet you found when you gave me back mine?"

"Huh?" said Birdie.

I didn't blame her. This was impossible to follow.

"And," Snoozy went on, "who's this *they* that's gonna be askin'?"

"Well," Birdie said, "it could actually be my mama."

"Whoa. You want me to lie to your mama?"

"No," Birdie said. "But it's not exactly a lie."

"On account of what?" said Snoozy.

"On account of other things I can't go into right now."

"Hmm," Snoozy said. "You in some kind of trouble?"

"No. Not really."

Birdie thought for a bit. Snoozy put his wallet away and yawned. He was a great yawner, almost in my class when it came to how wide he could open his mouth.

"What do you think about the sheriff?" Birdie said. "Is he smart or not?"

"He's the law," Snoozy said. "We have a saying about the law in the LaChance family."

"You do?"

"Sure thing. We have all sorts of sayings about all sorts of stuff. For example, 'Don't work too hard' and 'Always leave room for dessert.'"

"And about the law?" Birdie said.

"'Stay away from the law.' That's a LaChance family— what would you call it? Rule for a better life?"

Birdie was about to say something, but at that moment the phone rang. Snoozy reached for it, knocked it across the counter, gathered it up, and said, "Gaux Family Fish and Bait, Manager LaChance at your service." He listened. The voice on the other end came through sharp and clear. "Oh, hi, boss," Snoozy said. "How—" Grammy's voice rose. Snoozy held the phone away from his ear.

"You're not the manager! How many times do we have to go through this?"

"Uh," said Snoozy. "Makes the customers feel important, doncha think? To believe they're dealin' with the manager?"

"Bull pucky!"

"Never happen again. Anything else I can do for you?"

"Is Birdie there?" Grammy said.

"In the flesh."

"Put her on."

Birdie took the phone, held it to her ear. Grammy lowered her voice till I could no longer make out the words. Birdie listened, said, "Yes, Grammy," "I will," "Sure you're all right?" and "Bye, Grammy," and then hung up. She turned to Snoozy. "Water pump problems. Grammy's going to stay overnight down at Roux's boatyard while they fix it, sleep on the boat."

"Uh-oh."

"But she sounded pretty happy. It's an easy fix and they caught a twenty-five-pound striper, so the customer's happy. She, uh, wanted me to ask you when was the last time you cleaned the strainer."

"The strainer, huh?" Snoozy rubbed his chin. "Is that the thingy that keeps all the crud outta the pump?"

Birdie nodded yes.

"I'll have to think." His face went still for what seemed the longest time. At last he said, "You found someone else's wallet, not mine?"

"What's that got to do with any—" Birdie stopped herself, then sighed, took the wallet out of her pocket, and laid it on the counter.

"Nice-lookin' leatherwork," Snoozy said. "Saw one of

these in a catalog." He flipped open the wallet, took out the driver's license. "Preston Richelieu, huh? Ain't he the quarterback of the Hornets?"

"*Woo-woo*," said Birdie in a strange low voice, even angry. Angry: But at what I didn't know.

"What are you gonna do with it?"

"Return it. But I don't want to see him. Or anybody in his family."

"The Richelieus, huh?"

"Yeah. And what's with his middle name?"

"Pardo?" Snoozy said. "A pretty common last name up the bayou—Cleoma way, and west of that. Sometimes people put a family last name in the middle, keep it going. Like say my mother's name was Smith—I'd be Snoozy Smith LaChance."

"Your middle name is Smith?"

Snoozy shook his head. "Just an example. My middle name is actually Chance."

"I don't understand. Your mother's name was Chance?"

"Nope. Baldwin."

"So where did Chance come from?"

"Search me."

"And what's your real first name, Snoozy?"

"I'll never tell," Snoozy said. "As for the wallet, why don't you just go over to the upper dock and toss it on that boat of theirs—*Cardinal* or whatever the heck they call it?"

"Wow!" Birdie said. "That's genius."

"I do what I can," said Snoozy.

We walked back up the bayou path, past Trixie's Café, now closed, and came to a series of boat slips, most of them empty. Late afternoon now, quiet, the air heavy, tree shadows lengthening across the water. There was no one around. We came to *Cardinal*, a big boat, red and black, lying still in the very last slip. Something moved under the water not far away, making ripples.

We stood on the dock beside *Cardinal*, a raised dock, meaning we were slightly above the gunwales, *gunwales* being one of those nautical words you can't help learning when you live with a family like Birdie's. *Cardinal* had a big bench at the stern and two rear-facing fishing chairs. At the bow was the roofed-over cabin with the control console in the middle. Between the fishing chairs and the console was a stretch of empty deck. Birdie glanced around. No one to see. So now was when she was going to toss the wallet onto the deck, as Snoozy had said, right?

Wrong. Well, partly right and partly wrong. First, Birdie did toss the wallet onto the deck, where it landed in very plain slight. But then, after a pause, she turned my way.

"No poking around, Bowser. But also, no loose ends. How could a quick look-see do any harm?"

I couldn't come up with a single answer. We hopped aboard, side by side.

"But quietly, Bowser, quietly."

Oh, no. Had my landing been less than silent? How humiliating! The only way to deal with humiliation was to forget it at once.

twenty-one

WHAT HAD BIRDIE SAID? A QUICK look-see? As for what we could do after that, I had an idea of my own. How about taking *Cardinal* out for a spin, seeing what this baby could do? What's more fun than a boat ride? I leaned in against Birdie, hoping to somehow get my idea across.

"Cool it, Bowser."

We moved toward the stern. Things were very tidy, the way they should be on a boat, according to Grammy. "No clutter at sea!" I'd heard her say that plenty of times, including once or twice as she flung some knickknack over the side.

Birdie raised the cushions that covered the stern bench. Underneath was for the storage of all the usual stuff: life jackets, ropes, foul-weather gear. She lowered the cushions and we moved forward to the console, with all its dials, instruments, levers. Birdie opened the little cabinet under the panel of dials, took a quick glance inside, and then we continued on to the covered cabin in the bow.

A padlock hung on the door to the cabin. Birdie tugged at the lock but it didn't give. The door was one of those slatted things, like window shutters. Birdie peered through. So did I. All I saw were shadows, but I smelled Vin Pardo's limey aftershave. That seemed interesting to me, although I couldn't figure out exactly how. And what was this? I also smelled Bonnie? Was she in there?

"Bowser! What are you growling about? Didn't I say we had to be quiet?"

I searched my mind, found a vague memory of that. Quiet? Was that what Birdie wanted? Done! From this moment on I would be invisible, at least in terms of sound. What a confusing thought! I found myself panting.

"Bowser!"

Then there was nothing to do but give myself a good shake, the kind that flaps your ears and rattles the insides of your head. Nothing feels better than that, and as a bonus it sets you up for a fresh start. We walked back to the console and Birdie reopened the little cabinet.

"Maybe there's a key to the lock," she said.

She knelt down and studied the insides of the cabinet: suntan lotion, bug spray, charcoal bag, lighter fluid—all their smells constantly in the St. Roch air. But no key. Birdie pulled open a small drawer. Inside were some papers. Birdie looked them over.

"Ownership papers," Birdie said. Her eyes went back and forth the way human eyes do when reading is going on. "*Cardinal*, a thirty-five-foot blah blah blah owned by . . . by the Cardinal Fund? The Cardinal Fund, Bowser? What did Mr. Volk say? Drea's dad lent ninety-five thousand dollars to something called the Cardinal Fund?"

Birdie's eyes did some more back-and-forthing. "The Cardinal Fund, president Merv Richelieu, treasurer Miranda Pardo Richelieu—Pardo? Preston's mother has Pardo for her middle name, too? But don't women sometimes—" Birdie flipped through some more papers and then something at the bottom of the little drawer caught her eye. She took it out—a photo album with a plastic cover. We had one a lot like it on *Bayou Girl*, filled with photos of happy customers and their fish.

Birdie opened the photo album. I looked over her shoulder. The photos were kind of like ours—smiling humans and dead fish—except that the smiling humans in these photos were usually Richelieus, sometimes alone, sometimes together: Merv the dad, Miranda the mom, Preston the kid. Lots of smiling, but all their faces had something hard in them, at least in my opinion. Miranda had the biggest smile but also the hardest face. Did she remind me of someone?

Birdie turned the page. And there was Preston standing in the stern and holding up a big fish, so big that another dude was helping him. I recognized that other dude right away. At the same time I felt Birdie holding her breath. The helpful dude was Vin Pardo.

"Oh my god," Birdie said. Then her gaze went to some writing at the bottom of the photo. " 'Fun times! Preston with his uncle Vin.' "

Birdie looked at me. "How did I miss this, Bowser? Vin Pardo is Preston's uncle. That means they're brother and sister, Vin Pardo and Miranda Richelieu, and her maiden name must have been Pardo." Birdie leafed back to a photo of Mrs. Richelieu and a fish. "They even look alike, her and Vin. So . . . so what's going on? Had Drea already figured all this out? Did she break into both places? But why—"

A car door slammed shut, and not far away. Birdie froze. I heard voices, a man and a woman.

The man said, "You got greedy."

The woman said, "Look who's talking."

Then came footsteps, headed our way, first soft and swishing through grass, then harder and thwacky on wood—wood like the planks of the dock, for example. Birdie glanced around, her eyes wide and panicky. What was she looking for? I had no idea. All I knew was that I'd heard those voices before, the day Birdie and I paid a visit to the Richelieus' place, where I'd had a pleasant interlude in the backyard, if I remembered right.

Birdie half rose, her heart beating so loud I could hear it. She didn't want these people to find us aboard *Cardinal*. I got that part, no problem. For a moment, I thought we were going to jump over the side and swim for it. Then Birdie noticed a hatch cover on the deck, toward the stern. She scrambled over, raised the cover, and hissed, "Bowser." But I'm a world-class scrambler, had actually reached the hatch at the same time, or even slightly ahead of her.

"Me greedy, Miranda?" the man said, way closer now. "I know when to stop. That's the difference between you and me."

We gazed down through the hatch and into the engine well. We had one a bit like it on *Bayou Girl*, except not so roomy. The engine—a big complicated metal thing—took up most of the space but there was an open area along the side. Birdie and I dropped down into that empty pocket. She grabbed a ring on the inside of the hatch cover and pulled it closed. Everything went black. We huddled in the little pocket of the engine well, pressed close together. Birdie raised one of my ears, put her lips right against it, and very softly, barely a sound at all, whispered a long "Shhhhhhh."

I wondered what she meant by that. Then, just as footsteps hit the deck right above us, I figured it out. Birdie wanted me to be quiet. Done!

Footsteps—a man in sneakers, a woman in sandals—moved across the deck in our direction. The woman said, "You've got greed confused with normal ambition."

"I'm tired of hearing that line," said the man—Merv Richelieu, Preston's dad, if I was piecing this together right. "And you stole it from your brother in the first place. I'm so sick of—"

"Shut up. What's that?"

"What's what?"

"You're practically standing on it."

Birdie's hand tightened on the fur at the back of my neck. There was some more movement up above, and then Merv Richelieu said, "Huh? It's Preston's wallet."

"Let me see it." That was followed by a sort of grabbing sound and then Miranda Richelieu said, "What is it doing here?"

"Search me," Merv said. "Hey! Think he's on board? Preston! You here?" Keys clinked, sneakered footsteps moved toward the bow, more clinking, and then a door squeaked open. After a pause, Merv said, "Nope. No one here."

"Why would he be here?" Miranda said.

"Maybe hanging out with Solange Claymore. What does he see in someone like her?"

"Figure it out." I heard the *tack-tack-tack* of a sharp fingernail tapping at a smartphone screen. "Hello, Preston?"

272

Miranda said. "Are you missing anything? No? Not that you know of? Well guess what your father and I found on the boat—just lying on the deck in broad daylight." A pause, and then Miranda snapped, "Watch your mouth! What we found was your wallet. Any idea what it's doing here?"

A silence.

"No idea?" Miranda went on. "When was the last time you were on the boat? This morning? What were you doing here this morning?"

"I told you the answer to that already," said Merv.

"Don't interrupt! What was that, Preston? Out for a run and you took a short break on the boat? Since when do you run along the bayou?"

Now I could hear Preston's voice, tiny but talking fast.

"Yeah?" said Miranda. Then more of tinny Preston. "Uh-huh," said Miranda. "Uh-huh. Uh-huh. Well, just be more careful in the future. See you at home. Six on the dot. What was that? Her? No, I haven't. No sign of her around here. Why do you ask? Yes, I know she's a troublemaker, but is there something specific? No? Okay, see you tonight." I heard a soft plop, the sound a phone might make getting dropped into a purse.

"He says he went for a run," Miranda said, "stopped here for a—"

"Caught that part," Merv interrupted. "Who were you talking about at the end?"

"Birdie Gaux."

"What's she done now?"

"I don't know," Miranda said. "Preston was just asking if we'd seen her around here."

"What would she be doing around here?"

"I couldn't tell you why the little witch does anything."

Little witch? I knew witches from a horrible Halloween, back in my less happy life before Birdie. Whoa! Had Miranda Richelieu just called Birdie—my Birdie—a little witch? I did not care for that, not one bit.

"What's that sound?" Merv said.

"I don't hear anything," said Miranda.

But I did: a kind of low growl, very near and—I felt Birdie's hand, gentle but firm, right over my muzzle. A double realization hit me at once: The growler was me, and this was not the time. I got a grip, and fast.

"Sounded like something down in the engine well," Merv said. Footsteps moved closer. "Hope it's not rats down there." Knees cracked, like someone was bending down, right over our heads.

"Not when I'm around, for heaven's sake," said Miranda. "You know I can't bear the sight of rats."

What was this? Rats, down here in this pitch-black well with me and Birdie? I wasn't fond of rats myself, but I smelled none. Witches and now rats. My takeaway was that the Richelieus were wrong about all sorts of things.

"In fact," Miranda went on, "I've changed my mind—I don't even want to go out now."

"No boat ride?"

"I'm not in the mood."

"Okeydoke," Merv said. "But you've got no one to blame but yourself."

Miranda's voice went icy. "What's that supposed to mean?"

"The pearls," said Merv. "There was no need for the insurance play. That's what I mean by greed. And now the sheriff thinks we tried to pull off a scam."

"How dumb can he be?" Miranda said. "We took back the claim the moment Vin told us what he'd found on the little witch's camera."

"Dumb, maybe, but he's figured out the sequence of what went on—that was clear from his questions."

"So? What can he do? There's no claim. The pearls turned up in the laundry hamper, oh how embarrassing."

"But it got the sheriff thinking about the break-ins. Your brother always goes one step too far."

"You owe everything you've got to Vin. Who ponied up that cash injection when you were about to lose everything?"

"He did it for you. And then there's the matter of what he did to get that money."

"Toughen up," Miranda said. "Thirty-percent interest—Bolden got what he deserved."

At that moment, possibly distracted by the thought of ponies, I opened my mouth real wide. Sometimes when I do that, a little squeaky sound comes out.

"Hey!" said Merv. "You musta heard that—rats for sure." Footsteps, followed by a grunt, right on top of us. The hatch cover started to rise, letting in a narrow shaft of light. My eyes, used to the dark, couldn't see a thing. Then they could. And there were Birdie's eyes, so close, so terrified.

"Some other time, Merv," said Miranda. "I'm leaving."

Merv sighed. The hatch cover banged shut. Blackness returned. Footsteps moved away, off the deck, across the thwacky dock, through swishy grass. A car door slammed. Then another. An engine started up, made sounds that got fainter and fainter and faded away. After that the only sound was Birdie's heartbeat, light and fast.

We stayed where we were for what seemed like a long time before Birdie raised the hatch cover. Light came flooding in, weaker light now, and reddish, meaning sunset was coming. We clambered onto the deck, saw no one around, hopped onto the dock. Birdie looked at me. I looked at her.

"You're so brave," she said.

I licked her foot, all I could think of to do. She was wearing her blue flip-flops with the silver stars on the straps, the best human footwear I'd ever seen.

"I feel like I'm so close to understanding the whole thing," Birdie said. "I just need a little help." She got a faraway look in her sky-blue eyes. "Like . . . like from my dad."

Her eyes got misty. Poor Birdie, whatever this was about. I licked her other foot, and then we were good to go.

We headed down the bayou path, the water now reddish gold and thick-looking, and came to Gaux Family Fish and Bait. Snoozy was locking up.

"Hey, your mom's been calling."

"What about?"

"She's got a seven a.m. interview in Lafayette tomorrow, so she's staying there overnight. With Grammy's cousin Zinnia, heaven help her. And what with Grammy stuck on the boat, she wants you to sleep over at Nola's. She already called Mrs. Claymore. It's all set."

Back in our bedroom, Birdie started packing. We were going on an overnight trip to Nola's place? I could hardly wait! We'd had an overnight at Nola's once before. This time there'd be no gnawing on the legs of the Claymores' heirloom piano, whatever *heirloom* happened to be. You can trust ol' Bowser! Birdie was sticking a treat or two into her backpack, when someone knocked at the door.

Whoa! A man—I could tell from the sound of the knock—had managed to get right to the door without me knowing? And me in charge of security? I barked an angry bark, angry at myself, mostly.

"Shhhh."

Birdie went to the window, drew back the curtain a tiny bit, peeked out. I crowded in and peeked out with her. The sheriff's cruiser was parked out on the street. We backed away from the window.

"Shhhh," Birdie said again, just before a second knock, more powerful than the first.

"Hello? Anyone home? Aside from Bowser, I mean. Birdie? You in there?"

Birdie stood by her bed, totally still. I stood beside her, the same way.

"I'd like to talk to you, Birdie. If you're home, I'd really appreciate it if you let me in."

Birdie's hand, not quite steady, rested on my back.

"Maybe I've mishandled things when it comes to you, Birdie. As for whupping Rory, nothing like that ever happened. Not what you'd call whupping, maybe just the occasional spanking. But my fault for leaving the police radio where he could hear it. Too much to expect for the boy to . . . In any case, that's not why I'm here. Are you inside, Birdie? Hearing any of this? I've come about Drea. There are some new developments."

The trembling in Birdie's hand ramped up. In fact, her whole body was shaking. But she stayed where she was.

"Maybe you're not there. Maybe it's just Bowser, uncharacteristically on his own. But, Birdie, you'll want to know that your instincts about Drea were right. I heard from the medical examiner an hour ago. Let me in and I'll tell you."

We stayed put.

The sheriff sighed. Maybe sighs from outside the house are impossible for Birdie to hear, but I caught them. "Drea had no water in her lungs, Birdie. That means she didn't drown." The sheriff cleared his throat. "She was killed on dry land. Murdered. The ME found a very thin indented mark on her neck. He thinks she was strangled, possibly with a guitar string. I . . . I thought you'd want to know. I expect you have some questions."

Did Birdie have questions? I had no idea. But she didn't speak a word. The sheriff sighed again. I heard him move off the breezeway. Then came the sounds of him getting in the cruiser and driving away.

"Just a spanking, Bowser? Would Rory have even mentioned it if that was all it was?"

twenty-two

BIRDIE WAS DROPPING HER TOOTHBRUSH into her backpack when the phone rang in the kitchen. We went to answer it, Birdie doing the actual talking. I stood right beside her, easily hearing Nola on the other end.

"Hi, Birdie."

"Hi."

"You're sleeping over at my place?"

"Yeah."

"Want me to come get you?"

"Why would I want you to do that?"

"You sound a little funny."

"Funny how?"

"I don't know—scared or something."

Birdie's grip tightened on the phone. "I'm fine," she said. "We're on our way."

"See you."

"Bye."

Birdie hung up. We went back to our bedroom. Birdie picked up the backpack and then—and then let out a huge sigh and sat on the bed, which was not what I expected. After that came another surprise. Birdie shifted around and lay down. Lying on the bed? Wasn't it a little early for that? And weren't we sleeping over at Nola's? I could hardly wait to get to that piano—no, Bowser, no. I put that out of my mind, once and for all, and hopped up onto the bed beside Birdie. If it was time for sleep, I'd take a crack at it. I closed my eyes and immediately saw the Claymores' piano. I opened my eyes back up.

Birdie's eyes were open, too. She was gazing at the ceiling. Right above was the vent where she'd hidden the photo of Miranda and her pearls. Then she'd taken it out and given it to the sheriff. I tried to put everything I knew about the pearls into one tidy package and got nowhere. In fact, I had the feeling of going backward, knowing less and less instead of more and more. Ol' Bowser was cool with that! I snuggled closer to Birdie.

She rested her hand on my side. "No loose ends," she said. "No loose ends. But all we've got is loose ends."

Was this about her sneakers? She wasn't even wearing them, still had on the flip-flops. So we had no worries in the loose ends department. But Birdie didn't seem right to me. She looked hot, like she wasn't feeling well, her forehead damp, her cheeks flushed.

"Grammy says I'm like my dad, but if that was true

wouldn't I be able to figure this all out?" Birdie went on gazing at the ceiling vent. At least her eyes were aimed in that direction. But they had a faraway look in them, so maybe she wasn't—

All at once she sat up, so fast it scared me. "Bowser! I've got the craziest idea!" She bounded off the bed, out the door, and down the hall to the kitchen. She turned out to be a pretty good bounder, but when it comes to bounding, me and my kind are in a class of our own. So it was no surprise that I reached the kitchen first, and was already waiting by the door when Birdie flung it open. We raced outside, across the breezeway—where the smell of our snaky friend was stronger than ever, really something I had to investigate as soon as I had time—and headed into Grammy's side of the house.

We burst into Grammy's room. Birdie peered up at Grammy's ceiling vent, the one where Grammy and I could hear fluttering, but Birdie could not. How Grammy hated that fluttering sound, although it didn't bother me. I remembered her shoving the broom in that vent in a very angry way. I always kept my distance when Grammy had a broom in her hands. Not that she'd ever do anything bad to me, but why tempt her?

"Do you see, Bowser?" Birdie said. "It's like a test if we are like each other, me and him. When I had to hide something, where did I put it? And what if when he had to hide something, his mind worked the same way? Don't forget he was in this house before he died, Grammy away on the boat. Kind of like now. Do you see where I'm going with this?"

I most certainly did not. Meanwhile, exciting things were happening, involving the chair from Grammy's desk, Grammy's bed, and Birdie climbing way, way up. We were playing this game again? Who was luckier than me?

"No, Bowser, don't—"

CRASH.

Oh, the fun we were having! Hurry, Birdie, hurry! Get that chair back on the bed so we can clamber back on top together and—

"Bowser, sit!"

Sit?

"On the floor, not the bed." On the floor? But how could I play the game while sitting on the floor?

"If you don't sit, I'll have to put you outside."

Outside? Had I ever heard anything worse? I sat on the floor, as close to the bed as I could get, and not actually sitting if sitting meant you had to have your butt right down.

Birdie got the chair set up on the bed, climbed up, reached high, and got one hand on the grate to the vent.

"Now I hear the fluttering, loud and clear. Sounds like . . ." She poked her fingers through the grate. "I feel something but I . . . Maybe if I give it a little tug . . ." Birdie's fingers curled through the squares in the grate and she gave it a tug. Not a hard tug, but the grate popped out and Birdie lost her balance, Birdie, grate, and chair all tumbling down onto the bed. And that wasn't all. One more thing also came tumbling down. It landed smack-dab on Birdie's chest. She took it in her hands, eyes wide.

"The notebook!"

Birdie gazed at the notebook like it was something amazing. It did not look amazing to me. It looked like the notebook Grammy kept in the kitchen, the one with all the phone numbers inside, even though Birdie told her she didn't need it, the phone remembering all the numbers by itself. Or something like that. Way over my head. The point was that this notebook that had fallen out of the vent was just a plain pocket-size paper notebook with spiral rings along the side, nothing special. Birdie sat up and opened it.

"This is his handwriting," she said, her voice strange, so soft, almost nothing but a breath. "It's . . . it's strong, Bowser. All the letters are strong." She turned a page. "He writes little notes to himself—'flowers for Jen. Weekend at the beach? Check if Ma's free to watch Little Miss Fearless.'"

284

Birdie glanced my way. "Little Miss Fearless—do you think he meant . . ."

She went back to the notebook, turned another page. I felt a small breeze, smelled the outdoors, had a notion that we'd left the door open to the outside. An outdoor breeze for sure, carrying the usual outdoor smells, plus the scent of our snaky friend. Birdie's eyes went back and forth, back and forth. Then she went still.

" 'Theory of the Bolden Case.' Oh, Bowser!" She held the notebook with both hands, neither of them quite steady. " 'Bolden—developer—but money lending at 30%'s his real biz. 95k last Sept. to Merv and Miranda Richelieu of Cleoma. Imp.—she's a Pardo. Resort hotel project in Biloxi—financing fell through. 95k plus 30% due year from loan. Check out crazy bird-watcher with apt. on Friedrichs Avenue.' "

Birdie looked up. "Friedrichs Avenue? Wasn't that near where they found Mr. Bolden's body, floating in the river?" She turned another page.

" 'Not crazy, but dementia, poor thing. Loves pelicans. Takes thousands of pictures of them, including Exhibit A. She didn't notice the non-pelican part, even when I pointed it out.' "

"Exhibit A?" Birdie said. "What does he mean?" She turned one more page and . . . and a photograph fell out.

Birdie picked it up, read something along the top. "'Exhibit A.'" Then she gazed at the photo. So did I. A pelican stood on a lamppost, a wide river in the background. Under the lamppost stood two men. One was twisted around, his face not showing, maybe starting to fall. The other man had a gun in his hand. You could see the flash. You could also see his face, with its thin, dark mustache, and that golden dome of hair.

"Oh, Bowser, do you see what this means?"

I did not, but somehow I knew it had to be very important. I blocked out everything so I could think my very hardest, and that was how I was—blocking and thinking—when a voice spoke from the doorway of Grammy's room.

"It means nothing good for you."

Birdie and I both wheeled around. There in the doorway stood Vin Pardo. I hadn't heard him? I hadn't smelled him, hadn't heard him, had let him come into our house? This was the worst moment of my life.

Birdie rose. I stood right beside her. Together we were unbeatable. Now my job was to make sure that was true. "You killed my father," Birdie said.

Pardo shook his head. "I think of it as self-defense."

"Self-defense? You shot him in the back of the head."

"He was going to take me in for the Bolden . . . matter. There's a death penalty in this state, in case you didn't know. Making it self-defense in my book. And a blood-sucker charging thirty percent had best know how to back it up. Therefore, also a kind of self-defense."

Birdie tucked the photo into the notebook, clutched it in one hand. Her other hand was on my back. I felt it curl into a fist.

"And what about Drea? Was that self-defense, too?"

"She took a swing at me with her guitar," Pardo said. "So I'd have to say, yeah. Self-defense. And all so unneces-sary. If it hadn't have been for that blogger . . . but Drea read it and then when she got hold of the safe-deposit box she . . . Well, you know the rest. You're a troublesome girl. When I got wind of your batty old granny getting stuck on the boat for the night, I set up the early morning Lafayette interview—clear that pathetic mother of yours out of the way, too. Skip the whole house-buying charade, cut to the chase. Weren't you supposed to be at a friend's by now? I should have known." He held out his hand. "I'll have that notebook. Just toss it over."

"You talk about my family like that?" Birdie stuck the notebook down the front of her T-shirt.

Pardo's eyes got real hooded and nasty. "Let's not make this unpleasant. Just give me the notebook and . . . and you'll never be bothered by me again."

"Ha!" said Birdie. My favorite human, no doubt about it.

Pardo's eyes got even more hooded and nasty, reminding me of snakes I'd seen.

Birdie tried to back away, but there was nowhere to go. We were right up against Grammy's bed. "Get out of here," she said.

"I surely will. But I'll have that notebook first."

Birdie shook her head. Just a small movement, but how much I loved her at that moment!

Pardo reached into his pocket and took out a gun. "The notebook," he said.

This bad man had a gun? He was pointing it at Birdie? And she was starting to tremble? Just a little, but I saw it. That trembling was unbearable to me. I charged. After that, everything happened real fast. Did I bound across the room? No question about that. Did I spring at Pardo? Definitely. But just as I was about to lay him out and lay him out good, he swiveled the gun in my direction, not quick enough to point at me, just quick enough to swipe the barrel across my face. I went flying into a corner, couldn't see right, tasted my own blood. Then came the sound of Pardo—a big, dark shadow—barging across the room. He lunged at Birdie, grabbed her, flung her over his shoulder, and ran down the hall toward the breeze-way door.

"No! No!" Birdie screamed.

I got to my feet, gave my head a shake—clearing my vision a bit—and took off after them. Maybe not taking off at normal Bowser speed, but at least I was moving. Moving and growling: Real bad news was in Vin Pardo's future.

Meanwhile, he was at the breezeway door, Birdie still over his shoulder, kicking and shouting. He flung the door open with one hand, burst outside, and started across the breezeway. And the door? It slammed in my face just as I reached it. I was in and Birdie was out? Out and in horrible danger? I howled. It was all I could think of to do. But in the middle of my howling, I happened to notice something about our door that I must have seen many times yet never thought about, namely how it had a window at the bottom and a screen at the top. Were screens something you could jump through? I'd never tried. Now was the moment! Ol' Bowser leaped the most important leap of his life, up and through that screen, ripped right through it.

I flew through the air, somehow howling and barking and growling all at the same time. And then—*THUMP!* I came down hard on Pardo's back. We all fell to the breezeway floor, fell in one big wrestling, fighting heap. The heap rolled and rolled, a heap that was all about kicking and scratching and biting, me doing the actual biting. I sank my teeth into the back of Pardo's leg and wasn't letting go, not ever. But how strong he was! With one hand he kept raking me across the face with that gun barrel, over and over, my blood flowing all over the place. And his other hand? He'd gotten it around Birdie's neck and was starting to squeeze. She wriggled and thrashed and squirmed, but got nowhere at all. Oh, the look in her eyes at that moment! Please let me forget. Like she was about to die. Please let me forget. But her eyes? When they started going glassy? There would be no forgetting.

Then came some noise from under the breezeway, an irritated kind of noise. A moment after that, our snaky friend put in an appearance. Was it long and thick, or what? You'd never want to see a snake any longer or thicker. You'd never even want to see this one, take it from me. It slithered across the breezeway floor real fast—just one or two lightning-quick slithers—and glided right over Birdie's face. The look in its eyes! The exact opposite of Birdie's. There was nothing in them I could understand at all. Oozing savage life: Let's leave it at that. The snake's huge triangular head passed right over Birdie's face, over Pardo's hand, still squeezing Birdie's neck, and then it opened its terrifying mouth, exposing those snaky fangs. Snaky fangs that it plunged deep, deep into Pardo's forearm. The rest of the snake, from the head down, seemed oddly relaxed. Crazy, but that was the scariest thing of all.

Pardo screamed a scream I never want to hear again. It shook the sky. He scrambled off Birdie, got to his knees,

290

batted the gun at the snake's head to no effect. Then he put his finger on the trigger, about to use the gun for shooting instead of clubbing. Which was when I snatched that gun away. The Pardos of this world shouldn't have guns. A no-brainer, in my opinion.

"Get it off! Get it off!" Pardo punched at the snake with his free hand, his eyes wild and bugged-out and red, face all twisted. At last the snake let go and slithered away, not back under the breezeway but across the driveway and toward a vacant lot, which was very considerate.

Pardo struggled to his feet. He glanced around, spotted the gun in my mouth, took one step in my direction, and grabbed his chest. Then came a kind of gagging, gurgling cry. He sank to the ground and didn't move again.

A heavy silence seemed to fall over the whole town. Birdie raised herself up on her knees, her face as white as bone. She was shaking and panting and crying, but she got it together to gently wipe the blood off my face. The shaking and panting and crying began ramping down. "Who's the bravest dog in the whole wide world?"

That was an easy one. I gave Birdie my most affectionate kind of lick.

Nola came running down the street. "Birdie! I saw a huge cottonmouth right on the sidewalk! What—" She saw the scene in our front yard and stopped dead.

Birdie rose to her feet. She stood straight and tall.

■ ■ ■

So many things happened after that! No way I can be trusted to remember them all or get them in the right order. I'm pretty sure someone said that the snakebite, although poisonous, hadn't killed Pardo. He'd died of a heart attack, brought on by plain old fear.

Birdie got in big, big trouble for poking around against Mama's orders. At the same time, everyone treated her like a hero, maybe confusing the kid. Mama's face shining with pride while she gave Birdie what for? Confusing to me, for sure. I myself didn't get in any trouble on the poking around issue, ended up being a hero and nothing but. Ever gnawed on an antler treat? That was just one of my rewards. And it came from Grammy!

The sheriff paid us a visit and explained how he'd arrested Merv and Miranda Pardo for being accessories after the fact in two murders. Merv had already confessed that Pardo had killed Birdie's dad up in Cleoma but taken the body to New Orleans just to be tricky, Pardo being a tricky guy. The kind of guy who'd fake a second break-in to put the sheriff off track. The kind of guy who'd pay back a loan with murder. Had Birdie's dad hidden the notebook because he knew he was in danger? Or because he was just that way? Mama said because he knew he was in danger. Grammy said he was just that way.

The sheriff also told Birdie he was sorry about a bunch of things I couldn't keep clear in my mind. "That's all right," Birdie told him.

Mama had been sorry, too. "What a fool I've been!"

"Oh, no, Mama! Don't ever say that. Don't even think it."

And Grammy had picked Birdie right off the floor— even though she was so old and not much bigger than Birdie—and hugged her tight. "Now I can die in peace," she said.

"That's a long, long time away, Grammy."

"Just thank you, darling," said Grammy. Was there a tear in Grammy's eye? Maybe just for the briefest moment.

What else? Mr. Santini had a cookout down at the campground to kick off his sheriff campaign and we were the guests of honor, me and Birdie. Junior Tebbets wrote a song all about me and Birdie and how we'd solved her dad's last case and done lots of other things that were already getting hazy in my mind, but she refused to sing it, so he just played an extremely long drum solo instead.

Rory hit a home run in his very last at bat of the season. He brought over a big bouquet of wildflowers that same day. The next day Junior came by with an even bigger one. Those bouquets bothered me after a while. I began making plans to get rid of them.

acknowledgments

Many thanks to my family for their love and just plain existence; to all the people at Scholastic, notably my brilliant editor, Rachel Griffiths, and the wonderfully supportive Alan Boyko and Jana Haussmann; and to my tenacious agent, Molly Friedrich. And there's no leaving out my tireless (although often caught napping) researchers, Audrey and Pearl.

about the author

Spencer Quinn is the author of the *New York Times* best-selling Chet and Bernie mystery books for adults. His first Bowser and Birdie novel, *Woof*, was also a *New York Times* bestseller. As Peter Abrahams, he writes the *New York Times* bestselling and Edgar Award–nominated Echo Falls series for kids. Spencer lives with his wife, Diana, and dogs, Audrey and Pearl, on Cape Cod, Massachuetts.